SIXTY YARNS

by

Michael Toia

VOLUME II

QUIJIMINGLE EDITION

JOKALYM PUBLISHING

Culpeper VA

JOKALYM PRESS
Culpeper VA

ISBN: 978-0-9600859-5-8

To my Family –
Daughters Lynda and Karen,
Sons-in-Law David and Jeff,
Granddaughters Hannah and Abigail,
Shadow and Akki,
And most of all,
To the one who presented all to me,
Joyce

Prologue

F or some reason work on an earlier similar book, *Frog Tongues*, [1] got a bit out of control and kept spawning additional stories. There needed to be a cutoff point, a point where a collection of those stories could be set to print and the book finished. *Frog Tongues*, as this work, is an anthology of the first sixty short stories, and this the next five dozen. They are relatively independent, and thus a reader may notice some restatement of facts or situations on reading either or both works. As formerly, each story can be read in five to ten minutes, and in any sequence: front to back, middle outward, or just thumbing through the pages. So relax and enjoy.

---

[1] *Frog Tongues and Other Recollections of an Old Patriarch,* Dorrance Book Publishing Co., Pittsburgh, Pa, 2016, ISBN No. 978-1-4809-3214-2

Contents

BOOZE

A team of radio engineers on assignment in Panama was tackling a problem noted by the Marines during WWII: radio communication through jungles was nearly impossible. The dense, wet foliage seemed to just soak up the waves and prevent their traveling far. The team was measuring "can you hear me now?" through the heavy growth. Their equipment, in portable transportation cases, included a gasoline powered generator for electricity. But a radio antenna was also needed to do the work.

The antenna was hoisted aloft by a small, helium-filled dirigible-type thing called a *kitetoon* that rose as a balloon in still air, yet flew as a kite in a good wind. Round balloons get blown about in a stiff breeze and their tether begins to drag on the treetops.

Daily their measurements continued. As night approached, they rewound the tether, brought the kitetoon back down and stored it safely under a net staked to the ground. Each morning it was checked and given a touch-up of helium, then allowed to rise back to the proper height so work could proceed.

There was a problem. Many days the overnight humidity rose oppressively. By sunup, heavy condensation covered everything, the kitetoon and its net included. So much water weighed the thing down that it often could not go airborne until nearing noon, when the day's temperature came up and things dried off a bit. The crew tried variously to remove the water with little success. Their field report held this open as a problem to be addressed and solved for future deployments.

An after-action conference was called. The valuable measurements were considered, discussed, and used to plan yet-to-come additional measurement campaigns. The problem areas were studied: recommendations for their solutions were drafted. And up came the problem of condensation on the kitetoon. Various solutions were considered, discussed, and cataloged.

One conferee, a chemist, offered this possibility. He stated that, in his lab work, some procedures produce an insoluble precipitate from an aqueous solution. This is commonly poured into a funnel lined with filter paper, allowing the water to drain away. To hasten the drying, a solvent – often ether, sometimes alcohol – is poured through the filter. This mixed with the remaining water, and both drained off. The solvent evaporated quickly, leaving behind a powder-dry material. He suggested carrying a supply of alcohol and a sprayer: spray the kitetoon. The alcohol would mix with the water, both drain away and fall to the ground, the remainder rapidly evaporating and leaving the kitetoon dry and flyable.

The team lead dashed this proposal, saying, "Had we that much alcohol in the field, it would have served a far more noble purpose."

Ahh, yes – the best laid plans …

FIFTEEN HUNDRED

A las, children mature and ascend to adulthood. Too quickly comes the time to complete their schooling. So it was with our two. Family vacations in their later high school days took on the task of visiting institutions of higher learning. Mom and the girls spent many hours perusing college catalogs and literature, books and articles on which school offered what, the girls trying to decide on a major course of study that would lead to their career paths. In retrospect I must say they rather both surprised us as to their career choices. We did not see it coming.

There were visits to the several nominee campuses. Mom and I took the two to our own alma maters, excellent universities just a short walk from each other in the Pittsburgh area. We visited campuses of several state schools and out-of-state universities as well. And for whatever reason, our elder just seemed to "click" with a university far from home: Baylor, in Waco, Texas. And as her college years came, it was off to Waco, several states distant.

Mom, younger daughter and I accompanied our firstborn one fine week as she registered, was assigned a room in the freshman women's dorm, and moved in. It was August – far from the best month to visit Waco. The weather was, well ... warm. *Hot* is not quite the proper adjective. *Blazing* is. In but a few days I had consumed several gallons of soda from the dorm's vending machines while carrying various of her belongings up two flights of stairs, to the third floor dorm room.

There's an unexpected twist in this story. Most persons seek out the local "Coke machine" for soda. As did I. There *were* no Coke machines. There were indeed vending machines of the same description, but none sold Coca-Cola. All sold Dr. Pepper product. I came to realize then, that Dr. Pepper is to Waco as Coca-Cola is to Atlanta. Waco is its birthplace.

The city name brings to mind another image, the darker side of government, a macabre bit of history: "Reno's Barbecue," the awful destruction of the Branch Davidian compound well out of town, in the Northeast corner of the county. We have visited several times, reflected soberly on the seventy six or so foot-square red granite grave marker tiles flush with the ground, memorializing people executed, perhaps by accident, for their religious belief.

And why? The government decided they should arrest their leader, David Koresh, take him to trial, and imprison him. But they had already surrounded the compound, out there on the Texas plains ranchland, so already had him in a sort of prison. They had constructed a guard ring about the property. All that was needed was to maintain that guard and keep him there. Unfortunately things got out of hand. Terribly so. But I digress ...

No. 1 daughter was finally installed in the dorm and began her education. She had no auto at the time. Nor was one seemingly required. But on completion of her freshman year, a compelling case was made that a car really *was* rather a necessity. To that end we shopped that summer and acquired a Dodge Neon, a pleasing pea green, her choice of both auto and hue. It has in the interim served her quite well. It's still serving, half way through its second decade.

The next summer led to August, and time to return to school. Her few additional belongings, a travel case and one for myself, were loaded into the Neon. We began a return trip, daughter and father, three days, off to Waco from Northern Virginia. Mom was concerned for our well-being. She would stay behind and tend to No. 2 daughter, yet in high school. Mom fretted. It was to be such a long drive, with many opportunities for harm. Her refrain, "It's a fifteen hundred mile trip!"

We began. The two of us, father and daughter, both radio amateurs, had installed a mobile ham radio "rig" [2] in the car, whiling away the miles, one of us communicating while the other drove. We spoke to fellow amateurs far and wide.

A drive down the length of, and beyond, the Shenandoah Valley brought us to the Virginia/Tennessee line, to the city of Bristol, half in each of the two states. To this day I have not a clue as to how its government functions, how the city services are provided, whether there exists one or a pair of mayors, etc. Tho I am curious about the matter, am not sufficiently so as to urge myself onto the internet to glean the answers.

An overnight stop in Eastern Tennessee preceded an early morning departure. As she checked out of her room, I had already reported to the little Neon, and was listening on the ham frequencies. A group met daily on a particular spot on the dial, and we enjoyed intermittently talking to them as we moved from one state, one county to another. They in turn were trying to collect a sequence of ham contacts in as many counties as they could. It's a type of contest, called "County Hunting." So in a way we two were rather popular.

Daughter stowed her overnight bag and stepped into position to begin the first driving shift. We remained in the parking lot to complete a few contacts. As I had already spoken to the assembled radio friends, she took over. The conversations were short, friendly. A particular one went as follows:

---

[2] A transmitter/receiver, or transceiver, with external radio antenna. Similar to a CB set but with more capabilities.

The radio spoke: "Kilo Foxtrot Four Lima Golf Romeo, this is Victor Kilo Four Alpha Alpha Romeo. You are five by seven, Lynda."

The translation? Daughter Lyndas's amateur call sign is KF4LGR. The *Kilo Foxtrot Four* etc. is her call sign spoken in the international phonetic alphabet used for radio communication. The calling station was VK4AAR. I had already spoken to him a minute or so earlier, and Lynda knew his name from my contact. He gave her a signal report of 5 by 7, a reasonable value. Lynda answered: "Victor Kilo Four Alpha Alpha Romeo, this is Kilo Foxtrot Four Lima Golf Romeo. Roger, Alan. You are five by eight."

I entered the contact into our logbook. Lynda answered another handful of calls in a similar fashion, and as I entered them into the log, she began driving. Now, amateur call signs often begin with a letter or two that identifies the person's country. K identifies the United States. V usually indicates a Former British Empire country, VE indicating Canada, for example. Lynda knew that, and asked just where was VK? I told her to get a good grip on the wheel, watch her driving closely, and answered. "Australia." And it is. There we were, with a fifty-watt transmitter in the car, communicating with amateurs far and wide, halfway 'round the world and back.

Our journey continued thus, down the long haul westward through Tennessee, across the mighty Mississippi, and into Arkansas. The second evening we stopped short of Texas, at the border, in Texarkana.

The third morning off we went, into Texas, toward Dallas. The interstate runs West to Dallas, then another runs South to Waco. We chose a shortcut, across the diagonal of this triangle, off the interstates and along state highways. This led us through counties rather sought after by our on-the-air ham friends, and we made many short contacts driving through Limestone, Flintstone, and other counties. But finally we pulled into Waco, sought out our motel for the night, registered, then had a lovely evening meal. We had arrived. And in one piece, none the worse for wear.

We made our customary phone call back to mom, announced that we had arrived safely, and all was in order. We exchanged weather reports. Waco was at one hundred degrees Fahrenheit, in the cool of the evening. It had been up to a hundred thirteen that day, we were told.

Mom expressed her maternal concern. She said, "You drove fifteen hundred miles! You must be exhausted." She is wont to a bit or exaggeration. I had checked the odometer, and informed her that her estimate was quite over the mark.

We had driven but fourteen hundred ninety-seven.

JUST DUCKY

Weather would be seasonably warm, not to humid, ample sunshine, rain not expected until weekend – so the morning paper prophesized. The *Beetle Baily* cartoon of the day was enjoyed: our code-cracking crew made short work of the daily cryptogram while finishing their morning coffee, and were chewing away at the crossword puzzle of the day. This would occupy their attention on and off during lulls in the daily work load. We were an Army Signal Group.

Headlines boldly exclaimed the number one story of the time, so important that I should need to go to the paper's archives, dig out a copy, to remember whatever it was that history overran and gobbled up. It was a good time ago, circa 1961, the fall of the year. But one story, back a few pages, caught our attention. We were, at the time, soldiers of the Army, stationed in Georgia. The paper related this sequence of events:

* * * * *

Three Army officers at a Post well to the East, near Savannah, and along the coastal swamplands, had, the previous weekend, driven out into those swamps to do a bit of duck hunting. Such activities are permitted on Posts as part of off-duty-time entertainment. One needed proper licensing and permission from the Post Commander, of course, and the trio had same.

The remote roadways at that installation had been build up above normal water level by dredging, making a dirt lane easily navigated even by a standard auto, with fairly deep water-filled trenches on both sides. The three were returning to Main Post well before sunset, and as they passed a particular spot, there they saw it. An alligator, motionless, in the water, just off the road. Well! These three nee Yankees had not earlier seen a gator up so close, stopped their small truck, backed up a bit, and stared at the critter. It did not move. Not a twitch.

They then decided to step out onto the road for God-knows whatever reason. Prudence should have dictated otherwise, but was cast off, out of sight into the swamp, to be drowned by curiosity. They more closely examined their find. Yes – it was a gator, a fair-sized one at that, and quite motionless. They discussed the matter a bit. And an idea sprang to mind.

One of them reached into the bed of the truck, next to their small aluminum "duck boat," retrieved an oar. Another of the group retrieved the second oar. These they took roadside, closer to the sleeping reptile. One was lightly poked at the beast. No net reaction. Another poke. Still no action. The third one was the charm. This aroused the thing, annoyed it, and they came to find it contained a peck or two of teeth – large teeth. These were put to good use as the gator simply snapped at one oar, bit it in two.

The sudden activity was cause for alarm, and a mild flight response set in as our three intrepid, brave officers tried to make their way back inside the truck, as rapidly as prudent. Ahh, yes – prudence. It snapped back from where it had earlier been cast. But the gator was fast. It dashed from its mini-canal, gave a bit of chase, and took up a defensive position beneath the truck. No matter how the trio tried to return inside, the gator threatened every such feint. But they were not defenseless: there remained yet an oar in their arsenal.

Michael Toia

With that weapon they attempted to poke at their adversary, get it to depart from its position and return to the swamp. The gator remained annoyed, defiant. In short order it dispatched the oar, rendering the three rather defenseless other than to try to outrun the beast should it attack. But instead it thrashed about, bit off the truck's muffler, exhaust- and tailpipes, then turned its wrath upon the rear axle. This fare happened to be a bit more chewy. Teeth applied thereto began to pop out, the axle prevailed, whereupon the gator gave up its quest, crawled from beneath the truck and dragged itself back into the swamp.

* * * * *

Or so the story went – it was the explanation they later gave to the Post MPs who stopped them for having a faulty muffler, a noisy vehicle in the occupied areas of the installation.

The story said the three were Army officers, a Lt. Colonel, a Major, and a Captain. We had a really good laugh about it. Our company commander exclaimed, incredulously, "I don't believe it! Not a word! But any *three* of my Lieutenants … "

MARTICK'S

B altimore was then a delightful, interesting, friendly, and wonderful city. My love, Joyce, worked uptown as a computer systems analyst and programmer, one of the COBOL troupe of such. My workplace was some twenty miles distant, an engineering manager at a federal laboratory. Occasionally I would punch out of work, take a bit of earned leave, and drive to town where the two of us enjoyed a nice lunch and each other's company.

Many a time did we visit Lexington market, the city's block-and-a-half commons area that housed small stalls for merchants vending all sorts of comestibles: soft-shelled crab sandwiches, hoagies, fried fish, ice cream, and on and on. One particular shop, *Pollock Johnnys,* occupied two separate stalls and sold a wonderful polish sausage sandwich. In the first stall they operated a production facility behind a large glass wall, where could be seen the process of mixing the ingredients, grinding the product, stuffing the sausage skins, tying them into those long, chubby beads and hanging them to cure. Visitors would often stand by those walls, entertained by the procedures. Directly behind, across the wide aisle, was the other company stall, selling their product. More that once did we buy a sausage sandwich, turn about, approach the wall, watch the manufacturing process as we partook of lunch. Popular wisdom holds that, to enjoy the eating of sausage, one should not watch it being made. Bosh. We ignored it.

Joyce, of course, had lunch in the city far more than I, and with co-workers had scouted the environs in search of good fare. She had "uncovered," so to speak, an excellent restaurant offering French cuisine, her personal favorite. On a noonday get-together, we met outside her office building and drove to a small downtown parking garage, a two-story, open-air structure, columns supporting the upper deck, and a low masonry wall surrounding the lower. It was an honor-park facility. We sidled into space 83, exited and locked the car, walked to the entranceway where there stood a large, metal locker structure. I placed the requested two dollars into slot number 83. We walked toward the street.

A sidewalk led around the lot. The city was in rebirth, and along the street the old buildings of that block and others were boarded up, covered with weathered, gray, vertical planks about a foot wide. We approached the first such. Joyce stopped. She directed that I look over that masonry wall, into the corner of the parking lot. There rested an old, rectangular wire basked once used by milkmen of yore to transport their glass quarts to front doors of homes. She asked that I fetch it, set it down by her feet, upside down. Most curious! My sweets was always full of surprises, and this one I still recall many years later: it was quite unusual.

The request accomplished, she stepped upon the device, reached up the wooden boards, and there placed an index finger on a small button some several feet above street level. There was the faint ring of an old doorbell. She stepped down, directed me to return the crate to its former place, and we waited some few tens of seconds. And then, surprise! The boards moved. They were covering an old door, which was being opened from within. Most curious indeed. What was she getting us into?

We entered. And found a restaurant, décor being much as the earlier stainless steel diners, delightful aromas wafting in the air, the very essences of good, really good food being prepared. Our door-opener / attendant and Joyce spoke briefly. We were ushered to a table prepared for two, presented with the establishment's menu. We perused it, Joyce pointing out the various items and entrees, recommending this and that, as this was her specialty, and I, her student in the matter. She, of course, decided immediately on her favorite, and likely had pre-decided earlier that morning: French Onion soup, a bit of baguette and a nice salad. As for myself, I recall not what I ordered other than that it was delicious, very well above par for restaurant fare, among the best I had ever consumed. Yes, she had introduced me to another of Baltimore's finest, this my first visit of many, many more.

In the intervening years we have dined at many others offering the same venue: *Auberge Chez Francois, Le Pomme, Le Pappillon, La Madeline*, some approaching, but none exceeding, the fare of which we partook that day, at *Martick's.*

Martick's? Hardly a French-sounding name. But excellent indeed. One wonders: might it still be there? Among the best of Baltimore. It was so stated in an issue of *The Baltimorean*, a monthly magazine discussing events, what to do, what was where, in the city. The monthly contained a feature article, *The Best and the Worst of Baltimore*. Once, while seated in a reception area awaiting an appointment, I perused an issue. There, under *Dining* …

The Best: *Martick's. 214 W. Mulberry Street.* Not a surprise. I promptly forgot **The Worst**.

And, under *Lingerie* …

The Best: *Frederick's of Hollywood, Columbia Mall.* And indeed it was. I know. I know very well. Joyce, to my great delight, was a frequent patron.

And …?

The Worst: *Sonny's Surplus. Thirty-two locations.*

POLYLINGUALISM

E nglish was a common connectivity in our university project: our staff personnel came from many differing countries. We were somewhat as a miniature United Nations research group. Variously the graduate students had come from India, Columbia, Taiwan, Egypt, South Africa, and a few from the Unites States. As the project Research Engineer, I spoke what is generally regarded as neutral North American English, my few idiomatic constructs of early life having largely yielded to desuetude.

The differing accents somewhat hampered verbal inter-communication. At times idea interchange was slowed a bit thereby. In particular, our few researchers from India had quite some difficulty communicating with a few from Kentucky, the former accent a bit of a chippy, choppy syllabic structure, and the latter a slower Southern Appalachian drawl. On more than one occasion a pair, one Indian and one Kentuckian, would come to my office for assistance, as I could understand both accents, the Indian being the more difficult, and both parties could understand mine. I became the intra-English translator of the moment.

In the course of our research, two from South America came to me, not for translation assistance, but for technical advice on how to set up, instrument, and conduct a planned experiment. Estan, the junior member, was a grad student from Columbia, and Pli, the senior, a post-doctorate research assistant from Argentina. The conversation and planning began in English. Estan and Pli explained the basics of their concept. I assimilated it, a mental picture beginning to take form in all our minds.

We continued for some minutes, Pli addressing first Estan, then myself, alternately. But then, as he turned from me, Estan said something in Spanish. I did not, nor do now, have facility therewith, so said, "Whoa! Hold on – you're loosing me." Pli stopped, explained: "Estan and I share the same native language and thought our interchange would go more smoothly in Spanish. We'll switch back to English when we address you."

Alright. That worked well. We continued digging more into the details, ideas becoming more technically complex along the way. We more deeply taxed our brain cells. After an additional few minutes, Pli turned to Estan, in English. Estan simply put both hands up about chest height: Pli immediately segued to Spanish. And as he turned to me, in Spanish, I gestured the same: Pli smoothly segued to English.

By and by Pli's address to Estan, on signal, switched to French. Well, now – this actually improved the situation for me, as I had some facility with technical and spoken French. Estan was also comfortable: his Lithuanian-born wife had immigrated to France and her education had been in that country. Estan knew it well.

Pli turned back to me – yet in French. I am not *that* adept at the language, so gave the *switch* gesture. Pli segued to German. Hmmm? I was a student of German, both literature and technical, so was able to understand him rather well. I did not gesture, as the main point was to delve into the problem and come up with a viable approach, no requirement to do so in English or Spanish ... or any other specific spoken language.

Pli turned back to Estan, who had little facility with German. The *switch* gesture produced something I did not understand at all:

neither Spanish, German, French, nor English.   But I did not interrupt. Whatever it was, Estan could handle. And as Pli turned back again to me, still in that language, the gesture brought forth yet something I could not understand. I expressed a mild recoil, and with a bit of a surprised, concerned countenance, gestured again. Spanish resulted. I gestured yet again. Pli stopped, rubbed his head, then went through a sequence of seven to eight utterings that I caught in German, French *and* Engish: "What language am I speaking now?"

Estan and I had a good laugh: Pli stopped, was a bit fazed. We retired to the campus cafeteria for a cup or two of coffee, decompressed Pli, and continued the discussion later that afternoon.

STAMPED

The most memorable and enjoyable position I held was as an engineering manager, working for the Federal Communications Commission. That line of technical work, my vocation, grew from avocational interests. An amateur radio license earned in my teens had been upgraded to the top level, the *Extra* Class. To boot, both what then was called a First Class Radiotelephone license and a Second Class Radiotelegraph license had been earned. The first class radiotelegraph qualification required a six month position on board a merchant ship as a radio operator, and is a requirement that I, to this date, have not met.

The workday was a combination of highly exciting, avant-garde cutting-edge engineering, admixed with a more mundane need to manage everyday things, such as directing staff to handle overflowing toilets, malfunctioning air conditioners, and the like. But one of the highlights was to chair industry-government committees to address difficult engineering problems.

To keep abreast of the surging tide of engineering develop-ments, improvements and new adaptations, kept us on our toes constantly. Our lab went through such projects as adoption of color broadcast transmission standards, development of the cell phone system, international cooperation on communication satellite systems, communication standards and regulations, and the like.

Many proposals on how to adapt new engineering to communication systems crossed my desk. These often came from highly qualified engineering firms such as RCA, Motorola, General Electric, and the like. They were deeply thought out, intricate, and detailed. It taxed the brain at times to come to understand what the proposals actually meant, and how they might be adopted. There were, of course, unsolicited proposals in the mix, from well meaning citizenry suggesting possible changes and improvements to existing systems, or new systems that the proposer suggested be adopted. Some were worth note, but many technically were not.

One day a particular such came to my attention. While on the surface it appeared as a simple and elegant change to radio broadcast standards that would, at once, allow twice as many radio stations in the same spectrum, a good engineer would see beneath this glittering generality a flaw, a violation of basic physical science. The proposed system could not possibly work. It was, in fact, one of the worst I had encountered.

After reading it once, studying it a bit and checking my engineering texts and references, I actually had a good laugh at what it purported. It was impractical, impossible. I then reached into my desk and extracted therefrom a small rubber stamp seldom used. Two inkpads were part of my desk ornamentation, supporting various stamps to approve or reroute reports, etc. I opened the lid of the red pad, inked my stamp, and prominently, on the top front of the proposal, with a quick determined motion, smacked a stamp thereon. And thus it stood, in ¾" block lettering, a most suitable, succinct comment expressing my evaluation of the work. The proposal was then routed forward, up the chain of command, to the Chief Engineer, to whom our laboratory reported.

A wee bit of time passed. Duties included a weekly call to headquarters, and a drive from the lab down to Washington, DC.

On one such visit, I was asked to the chief's office. It was custom to touch base with the man himself, were he not in some meeting or another, and my presence was requested. I said a friendly "good morning" to his moat dragon.

Moat Dragon? Permit me to expound. The king sits on his throne in his castle, surrounded by a moat in which swims an ever-alert, fearsome dragon on patrol. No one is permitted entry without successful negotiation with said dragon. The term refers to the secretary of a top official, often in a cheerful manner indicating and respecting h/er/is power, occasionally in a derogatory sense. The former was always the case in our operation.

As I entered the chief's office, we exchanged a friendly good morning and customary opening statements. And I saw, prominently on top of everything, the report I had earlier forwarded, my red, block-letter stamped word BULLSHIT so glaringly evident. The chief pointed to it, said, "This is yours?"

I answered in the affirmative. He said, "You've a way with words. I studied the proposal. I couldn't find a more appropriate comment. Where did you get that stamp? I need one."

TREE LIGHTS

T he year proceeded. Christmas approached. Store decorations were so themed. Some sprang forth about the end of August. But that's rushing the scene too much. Thanksgiving, to me, is the key heralding event. While sitting and digesting that wonderful meal, then and only then do I give way to the coming holiday, and get into the spirit.

My spouse catches the mood better than I. With about two weeks to go we find ourselves visiting Christmas tree lots. She runs through the proffered mini-forest. I stroll slowly, letting her find the perfect tree. An occasional tag catches my eye. A hundred dollars! I'm in the wrong place! Wife reappears shortly, with the same reaction. We depart, go to another lot.

After several such visits, all rather pleasant, the aroma of freshly cut pine and fir in the air, a nice warming wood fire in a firepit adding its perfume to the air, we find our tree for the year, and its off to home, our selected beauty lashed to the roof of the car. Then it's off with it, the butt end placed in a bucket of water for a day or two.

The time comes. Our tree is manipulated, laid on its side, and its lower branches trimmed a bit to accommodate a tree holder.

We've become fancy of late and use a commercial, heavy, plastic device designed for the purpose. In younger days, when rather on the less wealthy side, we would simply put into service an old, left-over, five gallon plastic bucket that formerly held drywall compound or the like, place the tree's bottom in it, and pile fist-sized rocks inside to wedge and hold the tree upright.

Wife retires to a basement closet. Our lower level main room fills with boxes of assorted Christmas decorations. This continues throughout a week or so as she goes about hanging this there, that here, wreaths on the outside of the house. I assist as requested. We set up the tree in our living room. She brings forth the ornaments, angel hair, treetop angel, and strings of lights.

Ahh, yes – strings of lights. Some I believe we have inherited from our parents. I do rather recognize one such. These are the type with all bulbs in parallel. One burns out, it stays out. But it does not affect its mates. They remain lit. It's a simple matter to remove and replace the bulb, and not absolutely necessary to do so immediately. These strings are my friends. They are reliable, and may well wind up on one of our daughters' trees when we are dead and gone. They last.

Then there are others. Cheaper ones. Strings of one hundred (yes, actual count) small bulbs. The one I encountered ran the hundred into two series strings of fifty. One bulb burns out, its forty-nine string mates all go dark. At least the other fifty work: we are down to half power.

She turns to me. "Only half of this string works. Can you fix it?" Yes, a simple matter. Armed with a small Radio Shack multimeter, work begins at the dining room table. Remove the first bulb in the string. Check continuity from the plug to its socket. Find continuity. Replace the bulb.

Now go to the half way point in the string, to bulb number 25. Remove it. Check continuity. Find and OPEN circuit. No contact. So a bulb from there to the first is burned out. Put bulb 25 back into its socket.

Go to bulb 12. Repeat the procedure. Pull the bulb out. Check for continuity. Again find an OPEN circuit. No contact. So a bulb between there and the plug is burned out. Continue as above.

Finally find the burned out bulb. It's the second from the plug, bulb 2. Replace it with a good bulb. Go back to bulb 25 and check for continuity. OPEN. Another bulb is burned out. Repeat the above process to find the bad bulb. Finally achieve continuity from the half way point to the plug. Now go to the end of the string, bulb 50. Check continuity. OPEN. Repeat the process. Replace burned out bulbs.

The process continues. Aggravatingly, one check returns me to bulb 25, and the circuit is OPEN! No continuity. But it had been OK a bit ago. Repeat the process. Find a bulb that is not quite making good contact. Clean and reinsert it. Finally achieve continuity.

This nonsense continued well into the night. Finally, at about eleven PM, I came to a satisfied, desirable result, quit work, cleaned up the dining room table, and retired for the evening.

The day after was the Sabbath, Sunday. We had a nice breakfast, admired our yet-to-be-totally decorated tree, sat about the house a bit, then prepared for Church. At an appropriate time we departed, drove to our little chapel in the woods, greeted fellow parishioners, and settled down as service began. A hymn. A prayer. Some announcements. And we came to the "Expression of Joys and Concerns." I sat, thinking, then raised my hand. My turn came.

"I have a joy. Last evening I worked on a malfunctioning string of Christmas tree lights. I worked five hours, but achieved success and The Lord granted me comfort. I decided the whole thing, along with its 'Hecho en China' inscription, was a piece of junk, tangled it up and heaved it into the trash bin. Then I slept well. I'll buy a new string tomorrow."

I received a round of applause!

ADVICE

A few young ladies are part of our life, close, part of the immediate family: two daughters and three nieces. We knew them all from the time of their birth. They advanced to young womanhood. Young bucks came along, igniting my patriarchal instincts. It was my duty to care for these beautiful flowers, to protect, that they not be unduly hurt by the trials and tribulations of the world.

In the case of our immediate household, I stumbled across a trick that kept all but the most dedicated and serious young fellas at bay, and as a father I pass it on so others might find it advantageous. An evening approached, and daughter was cheerfully, a bit excitedly, preparing for a date. A young man would shortly appear and escort her out. The trick I describe occurred at first accidentally as the day's events advanced.

Dinner was over, the dining room table cleared of dishes and utensils, and there I sat, spread a layer of newspaper, and began disassembly of my shotgun. I had fired it a day earlier and it was in need of cleaning. Nearby rested the gun cleaning kit, bore cleaner, gun oil, a cleaning rod with brushes and a small quantity of cotton "gun patches" needed to finish swabbing out the bore. I wore older work pants and had removed my shirt, lest it be soiled with oil droplets, and addressed the task at hand in a vest-type tee shirt.

The doorbell chimed. Daughter was, as usual, upstairs in her room, prepping for her date with the assistance of mother, and her sister was off in another room listening to a CD or so. I was the obvious nominee to tend the door, and did so. A pleasant young man stood on the porch. He seemed taken aback a bit at the sight greeting him, and as I invited his entry, I shook is hand. Tho I had wiped it well, there remained nonetheless the feel and a scent of gun oil. The lad responded very respectfully. His eyes perused the scene, the living room, the large entranceway to the dining room, its table and contents.

I bade him be seated on the sofa and called to the daughter of the moment. As expected, she tarried a bit, so the lad and I talked politely in the interim. Daughter then began her descent from the second floor, witnessed the scene, noticed the slight aroma of gun oil in the air, and chided me: "Oh, dad – did you need to clean your shotgun *tonight?*"

Well, it needed cleaning, and everyone in the house was elsewhere, so it had seemed like a perfectly reasonably procedure at the time. Did I do something untoward? I though not. But then my spouse appeared as well, and exuded the body language suggesting that I should ought to have put off the task till another evening. Mea culpa.

But as life continued unfolding, I noticed young lads seemed a bit more proper and respectful in such a situation. I thereafter began simply *feinting* gun cleaning on selected evenings, some newspapers on the table with a disassembled pistol as a prop, massaged a wee bit of gun oil onto my hands and employed the latter to dab on a bit of the same as an ersatz cologne.

This seemed to exercise considerable control of the situation. Most boys, mayhaps of less than good intent, did not return for a second episode. Two did. They are my delightful sons-in-law today, two sons that I never before had, and respectful husbands of my daughters.

Michael Toia

I am an aficionado of movies, and find a seminal line in many of them. Who can forget Rhett Butler's famous, "Frankly, my dear, I don't give a damn!" in *Gone with the Wind?* It was the first such that stuck with me, and I delight in finding others, such as *Bruce Almighty's* "Remember, folks, behind every successful man there's a woman ... rolling her eyes."

As the daughters' romances developed and my sons-in-law-in-waiting got on toward betrothal, I presume my past actions had played an interesting part. Each in turn approached me, and sought my permission and blessing to grant the daughter's hand in marriage. I had not expected such respect but am deeply honored that each did so.

And as they did, I said, "You ask her. If she says 'yes,' then my answer is yes. If she says 'no,' then bug off." I added at that time a modification of my favorite line from *Clueless*, where the irascible father tells a young buck calling on his daughter, "You take damned good care of her. If you don't, I have a .45 and a shovel, and I doubt if you'll be missed!" The sons-in-law withstood this test, persevered, and are two wonderful additions to the family.

It came to pass that my three nieces married, each in her turn. I was not present for the first two weddings, as other duties and work called. Wife and I were present at the third and youngest's wedding. It was a beautiful church affair, with reception following at a hotel ballroom. The night wore on. I found myself in the lobby as the groom came by. We spoke a brief congratulations, and I rather instinctively delivered the ".45 and shovel" line. He promised he would take the very best care of her.

Some several years passed. Wife was on the phone with the niece. A request was relayed: put Uncle Mike on the line. Wife handed me the instrument.

After a brief hello and good wishes exchange, she asked, "What did you *say* to my husband on our wedding night? Something about a gun and a shovel? He's been concerned about that ever since." I was caught totally off-guard, and said simply, "Let me ask *you*: is he taking good care of you?" She answered, "Oh, the *best*!" I said, "Then tell him he has nothing to worry about."

Hmmm? My sons-in-law came to know my jocular nature a bit before asking for the daughters' hands, and took that into consideration. Unfortunately my new nephew did neither. He misunderstood, thought I was serious!

I'm so sorry. I don't even *own* a .45 …

It's a .38.

CHECK

A foray into entrepreneurship quenched our desire to become independent. The business returned sufficient cash to keep the wolf at bay, but its long hours and less than stellar performance did their trick: it educated us further into the realities of life. We might have stuck it out a while longer had God not graced us with two little babies at the time, and man graced us with quite expensive health care costs, for we were just an isolated quartet of individuals not eligible for membership in a larger medical risk pool as are large corporations' employees.

Further taxing of our financial position was brought about by theft from the business and our property. We were relieved of the possession of two small boats, a good deal of miscellaneous shop tooling, and a few thousand dollars' of inventory, the latter through the activity of a thief, who in the wee hours of one night broke into our small store. The incident required a closing for a day, taking of a complete inventory, cataloging what was missing, cleanup of a broken window and a general mess made by the event.

At the time we ran a video rental service. For a modest overnight fee we provided customers a video playback machine and movies of their choice. This provided a decent cash flow and carried much of the weight of our business. We maintained a fleet of six rental machines, most of them out on any given weekend, along with a video library of about four hundred titles.

The inventory revealed one missing machine and six movie titles, along with some other equipment. Ahh, yes – all the niceties of living in the Deep South, the "Bible Belt" of the southeastern United States. Never before had we encountered such thievery.

Three or so weeks aprez-theft we ran an ad in the local papers, listing the movie titles that were stolen, and offering a cash reward for information leading to the arrest and prosecution of the thief. And a week thereafter, we got a hit! A conscientious lady called, said she had seen just such offered for sale at a second hand thrift store about thirty-five miles to the east. We took her name and information, then discussed the matter with our chief of police.

Thursday of the following week the chief stopped in during a mid afternoon lull in business. His visit was not unusual. He was a customer of our video rentals.

He asked if I might lock up for a bit and step across the street. I did so. The chief opened the trunk of his car to reveal an exact copy of what had been stolen, and asked: "Can you positively identify these items as yours?"

We carried them to the store and set them on a table. I began by showing the chief my billing records from one supplier, and the important notation, "A541," as we were known to the supplier's computer. Then I took another of our rental machines, removed its cover, and revealed on the left rear of the machine's chassis, written in permanent ink, the notation "A541." I did a similar showing with a few of our movie cassettes. I said, "If what you brought has the same markings, then it is mine."

We removed the cover of the machine brought to the table from the chief's car. And there it stood: "A541," exactly as described. The same was found on the movie cassettes from the chief's car.

With that I proclaimed, "Yes, these are some of the items stolen during the burglary." The chief kept the stolen property as evidence for a while. And a bit later, search warrant in hand, he paid a visit to a property out in the county, whose barn contained myriad items: several dozen new tires, pickup truck camper caps, small boats, new tools, and on.

The owner's son was an upstanding member of the National Guard unit in town. And the next Saturday, late afternoon, several guard members left the armory to find their vehicles in the parking lot, up on blocks, missing tires, and in some cases, wheels as well. Tires do have serial numbers, and many were identified as stolen property and taken as evidence. Our thief was in the discount new tire business!

He was apprehended, taken to trial, found guilty, and sentenced to a four year prison term. We finally received our stolen property. But the whole experience, the lack of suitable rate of return on the business, the needs of our new two girls, led us to close shop, move out of town where I took employment at a USAF maintenance base. We moved to an adjoining state.

We sent the conscientious lady a check for one hundred dollars and a thank-you note.

The second post-move Christmas approached. Our little ones had the run of our rental house. Behind the sofa stood a very large bay window, and that space an excellent playpen area for the darlings. The grandmothers had come to stay for a week, celebrate the holidays, and enjoy the girls as well.

Christmas Eve I awoke quite early, sat up in bed, and suddenly exclaimed: "Good gosh! Christmas Eve! And I had made a promise that slipped away from me during the excitement of the previous week, the parents' visit, and preparing for the season.

We had a pile of leftover merchandise, several small battery operated toys, radios, flashlights, and such. About two miles down the road sat an orphanage, and I had but a few weeks' earlier called to ask if I might be able to help out by donating these leftovers for the children's enjoyment. The orphanage manager and I had agreed that it would be well appreciated. He gave me a nose count: how many girls, how many boys. I had earlier gone through our leftovers and picked one item for each, and had them in a few large shopping bags. But in the hubbub I had not delivered them!

Quietly I rose from bed, called the orphanage, explained the situation, and inquired: is it too late? Au contraire. They were planning a Christmas party that evening and timing could not have been better. With that I quickly did my morning routine, dressed, and went quietly to the garage, allowing the rest of the family to sleep in a bit. In short order I had my vehicle loaded, drove to the orphanage, and staff helped me unload. They thanked me profusely, and I them, for not only had our garage been thinned out, but I felt well with the Lord as perhaps some children might have a better Christmas.

A return to the house found everyone awake, starting morning activities, the grandmothers and wife preparing a nice, leisurely breakfast which one and all enjoyed. We lingered at the table, talking, enjoying each other and a bit more coffee. The two little ones retired to their playpen area. In a bit the elder of the duo excitedly shouted, "Mail Jeep! Mail Jeep!" The postman was at the road, making his rounds. It was approaching ten AM.

I left our company, donned a jacked and proceeded to retrieve the mail. And in the morning delivery an unusual letter came to light, from the county court at our previous residence. Hoo Boy! What trouble were we in now?

I opened it. A letter explained that our former thief was now on probation, and the state's law demanded restitution be paid. A check in the amount of two hundred fifty dollars accompanied the letter. Well! This was unusual, very welcome news, totally unexpected. We all marveled at how it had arrived on Christmas Eve. Really, now? And a thought, that small, metaphorical light bulb that appears above one's head, did so. I asked my wife: "Aren't they delivering mail twice a day this season? I thought the

TV reports had said so." For the past week the "Mail Jeep" did come, once in the morning and again later in the afternoon. She answered in the affirmative. I then said, "Excuse me. I'll be back in a bit." Wife asked what was so important that needed immediate attention. I stated an urgency to go to the garage and get together a second load of old inventory, then rush off to the orphanage for another delivery. After all, something from the Bible said a bit about giving and receiving back tenfold, and gave this as my excuse.

Horrors! The grandmothers laughed, but my spouse became quite peeved, scolded me, saying "It doesn't work that way!" I countered, saying something about *ye of little faith*. However, she prevailed, and I admit that I, too, had not *that* much faith, and was acting out a bit of a joke, which I thought then, and yet today, was a pretty good spur-of-the- moment concoction.

EDITOR

A s with most others, the engineering profession involves preparation of many documents, be they notes, memos, letters, files, reports, scholarly articles, or the like. Many an engineer or scientist finds navigation of the language a bit of a stumbling block, an often difficult task. It's said the average worker in the field has a vocabulary of approximately twenty-five hundred words, scores of those being technical terms.

For a reason I neither understand nor can explain, others had decided that technical writing is one of my abilities. *Why* escapes me. My best guess involves an early fascination with war surplus electronics materials and their manuals. A writing style noted therein became part of my fiber: the use of a particular grammatical structure in the manuals.

A point was made, no attribution as to its authorship. *"The radar was operated to effect target detection to fifty miles."* Who operated it? That was unimportant. The radar's capability was the point. This construction is called the *passive voice*. It permeated most of the literature that found its way into my presence and interest.

Perhaps another way to illustrate the structure is in reference to illegal activity, statements such as, "The goods were delivered" coming from the prohibition era. The two important points were that a product arrived as planned *and* no specific person was incriminated as a wrongdoer.

At one juncture several of us became involved in the development of a satellite earth station needed to provide new capabilities. *What* capabilities? Our team canvassed the so-called "stakeholders," those who needed the new satellite service and/or who would provide the funding for the project. We conducted weekly meetings, collected inputs from stakeholders, and began composing a "Users' Requirements Document." The procedure continued for a year and a half. In all, eighteen successive drafts of the document were assembled before stakeholders came to agreement that it did, in fact, correctly define and present all their needs.

Thereafter we embarked on preparation of yet another bit of officialdom, the "System Requirements Document." This, with copious uses of the word *shall*, detailed all requirements that the system must meet. Our team worked for about nine months, wading through six successive drafts until stakeholders again agreed that all requirements were properly listed and legally enumerated.

About halfway through the Users' Requirements, and all of the System Requirements phases, two talented young ladies were assigned to assist our team. They were technical editors. We provided the technical content. They saw to it that rules of the language were properly followed, assured agreement of subject and verb, provided consistency of present or past tense, undangled our participles, no-no-ed our double negatives, assured correct punctuation, and so forth.

I, being rather of old school engineering, expressed what the system was to do, without mention of to *whom* the task fell. Of course the passive voice structure appeared in approximately every third of my sentences. It was just a natural "feel" for how one express one's self in technical jargon.

The ladies referred drafts back to us, using the *revision* mode of editing software. We studied their corrections, and for the most part accepted them, taking care that the technical meaning and definitions were not altered thereby.

A famous story along these lines concerns Sir Winston Churchill and the London Times newspaper. The Times published one of Churchill's speeches, noted that he used a preposition to end a sentence with [sic]! They corrected that sentence so it ended not with the preposition. Sir Winston took umbrage at this affront, as it shaded the meaning of his speech a bit. His reply to the Times, now a famous statement: "This the sort of nonsense up with which I shall not put!"

One of our editors called attention to my writing. She indicated that it was a rather older, stuffy style, and modern usage requires use of active voice constructs. She said I used entirely too much passive voice: please adapt to use of active voice.

I considered the matter. After all, we deeply respected and relied on their talents, were appreciative of them, and knew their efforts rendered the document far more readable and legally binding.

I tried. I tried hard. It just did not come naturally to me, having to interject named nouns as those who *did* or *would do* such and such. I had difficulty adapting to this requirement but succeeded – in part. Whereupon, following the three rules of good message composition, *clarity, conciseness, completeness*, I answered her request thusly:

"It is done."

Weeks passed before she once again would *speak* to me, and then only after I had apologized, and had taken her to lunch.

We remained, in the end, on friendly terms.

FCC

Working for a highly regarded technical firm found me on a flight from SEATAC back to the Northern Virginia area. We had just finished an assignment on Badger Mountain, East of Wenatchee. My seatmate and I were chatting, he having just retired from the Federal Communications Commission, where we had worked together a decade or so earlier. In fact, at my insistence he had been hired as a temporary technical assistant on the Wenatchee job.

Discussion went to our FCC days, and a story from the lore of old, supposedly about an FCC engineer working along the US East Coast. He was a field inspector, visiting and checking the nation's radio and television broadcast stations. He traveled under cover. His auto, though registered to the US Government, carried "cover" plates to match the state in which he was working at the time. I'll call our friend Jay to simplify matters.

The story line follows.

*   *   *   *   *

Jay had been on the road for several weeks, working through the Carolinas, and into the tidewater area of Southeastern Virginia. Finally he was finished and headed home, and rather late one evening was cruising up US Route 13 through the Delmarva Peninsula. Having been on the road since morning, Jay was tired, but anxious to be home that night, and probably driving a bit over the limit.

And it happened. A police cruiser pulled up behind him, with one of those blinking bubble gum machines on its roof. The law! The local sheriff pulled him over. They conversed:

Sheriff: "Son, y'all drivin' a tad too fast. Limit's 55. Done clocked ye at 85."

Jay: "Oh, sorry, officer. I've been on the road all day and just anxious to get home."

Sheriff: "License an' regist'ation, please."

Jay complied. He took his driver's license from his wallet, and from a briefcase sitting on the passenger seat he retrieved the vehicle registration card, handed both to the sheriff, who studied them, then said: "Sorry to tell ye, you in trouble, son. This heah license is fo' District o' Columbia, and this regist'ation is fo' No'th Ca'lina. And you in May'land now."

Jay: "That's a problem?"

Sheriff: "Yeah. You in violation o' da tree-state rule."

Jay: "Three state rule?"

Sheriff: "Uh huh. Of wheah you is, wheah you drivah's license is issued, an' wheah you vehicle is regist'ed, two o' those gotta be the same. Step outta da cah, please."

Jay did so. He took the briefcase with him. He asked the sheriff to let him look into it. The sheriff was a bit concerned, but agreed. Jay and the sheriff went to the rear of the car. Jay said: "This is Maryland?" He riffled through the briefcase, and pulled out a Maryland license plate, squatted down, yanked the North Carolina plate off the auto ... it was fastened with Velcro ... and pasted the Maryland plate in its place.

Sheriff: "Now wait a minute, son. Y'all cain't do thet!"

Jay then pulled out a District of Columbia plate, and said, "This do then?"

Sheriff remained skeptical, became even a bit more agitated. Jay too. He was rather tired, and as is said, started to "loose his cool." So he pulled out a stack of license plates, from Florida to Pennsylvania. With that, the sheriff took him under arrest. He confiscated the briefcase, kept Jay's registration card and driver's license, and ordered Jay to follow him to the town police station.

They arrived, parked the autos, and the sheriff escorted Jay inside, told him to have a seat, and made a phone call. Shortly the local magistrate appeared, and began processing an arrest. Jay asked a simple question: "I would like to make a phone call." He was permitted to do so.

He called a number ... *the* number ... of the FCC watch officer. That position is manned constantly, weekends, holidays, always. Jay explained his situation. The watch officer asked for the number of the phone Jay was using, and the call ended. Jay hung up.

The magistrate then proceeded through the booking procedure. Name. Address. Charge: speeding more than ten miles over the limit. And while he was so occupied, the phone rang. Sheriff answered: "She'iff's office. She'iff Duncun speakin." There was a bit of a pause. Then:

Sheriff: "But, suh, this heah boy been speedin' an' got a satchel full o' stolen license plates ... yes suh ... yes ... yes ... ah unde'stands, suh ... right away, suh."

The sheriff hung up the phone.

Magistrate: "Who in tarnation wus thet?"

Sheriff: "The one pe'son who can fiah both of us. Let him
             go. Now."

With that, the booking procedure ended, Jay was given his briefcase, registration card, license, an apology, and a mild admonition to slow down a bit so he doesn't kill himself. Jay gathered his materials, said a polite thank you, goodnight, and left.

* * * * *

I had finished the story, said, "That's about the way I believe I was told. I often wonder if such tales are true." My companion said, "It's a good story. And the basic parts of it are all true indeed."

I was surprised, a bit elated in fact. "It is? It really happened?"

My buddy said, "Yup. And you *know* 'Jay.' Do you remember my deputy when I ran the Baltimore office years ago?"

I: "*Doc*?"

He: "Uh huh. Doc."

So some of these tales of the lore of old actually are based, in reasonable part, on fact, though as with any story, its telling and retelling causes meandering of the truth. But, as is said, "Never let the truth get in the way of a good story, and if it wasn't true, it shoulda been."

This one is. It's my story, and I'm sticking to it.

FORM

November ushers in open season for government employees. It affords them their annual opportunity to modify their health care plans. To do so, one now goes online, logs onto a particular web site, presents one's personal identification and passwords, and gains access to instructions identifying the many options. Health care for one? Family? Low option? High option? Vision and dental? Long-term disability care?

Then one need consider the various offerings. Washington DC area? Virginia? US wide? Foreign travel? HMO? PPO? Blue Cross? Kaiser? Aetna? The choices are various and plentiful, with differing costs per pay period: A single person saves money by not opting for family policy. An elderly couple saves by opting for a health care pre-tax Flexible Spending Account.

This year there was a new offering: Self plus one. We had been taking the self plus family option, to assure that my spouse would be covered by our plan. Our children are now adults, moved on, each married and starting their own families. They are covered by their spouse's plan. We need no longer cover them, and the new option purported to save expense. At any rate, they are now over twenty-six, no longer "Obamacare children," and no longer qualify for coverage under my work-provided plan. We wanted to elect this new option.

I sat at my computer, called up the appropriate web site, logged on, was authenticated with my proper password, and began searching for that option. Amazingly, it did not take long to satisfy my request, and there on my screen appeared a form, SF2099 or some such, standard form number two thousand and ninety-nine, ready to be addressed. It was well laid out, with clear instructions, and could be completed online by simply filling in data in various defined "fields." I began.

Name? It was entered. Address? City? State? SSN? Date of birth? And on it went, gathering information about the insured. It was easy to navigate the form and provide the requested data. The same was asked for the other to be insured, and all was provided. The form was easy to review, to check for accuracy or missing data, and such was done. Finally at its bottom it offered two options: SUBMIT or CANCEL. I chose the former, clicked on SUBMIT.

A pop-up message popped up: "Date of birth is a required field." It was easy to navigate back to the date-of-birth fields, one for myself, a second for my spouse. Both fields contained the correct data in the form-suggested format of mm/dd/yyyy. To be sure, I deleted and retyped the data in both fields, scrolled to the bottom and clicked SUBMIT.

The pop-up popped up again. "Date of birth is a required field." I repeated my former corrective actions, thinking I had made some mistake. I carefully entered the correct data in the requested fields, checked it twice, scrolled again to the bottom, and clicked SUBMIT. The pop-up popped up yet again, same incantation. I re-examined the form very carefully, and noticed that every field in which data was required was surrounded by some stylized brackets, sort of like [[and]]. Every field. Except one. Date of birth of insured. The brackets were missing.

No action on my part could submit the form. I opted to save it, seek help, and complete it at a later time. The form provided no option to SAVE. The only two were SUBMIT or CANCEL. And as SUBMIT did not work, *I* submitted and clicked CANCEL. I had now been on the web site about an hour, and was only slightly closer to achievement of my goal, having at least seen how to find and fill in the form, if only it worked.

The web page had a hot link to an assistance site. I clicked it. Another form popped up. It, too, asked for data: Name? Address? City? State? SSN? Date of birth? And on. It asked for the nature of the problem, in 100 characters or less. In my frustrated agitation the count was quickly exceeded. Some careful wordsmithing, with concomitant waste of time, finally satisfied the computer. *This* form was submitted. And this time SUBMIT actually submitted the form. I then exited the web page related to health care options and took to other profitable use of the computer.

An hour later an e-mail message popped up: new mail in my in-box. I opened e-mail, saw a reply from my assistance request. Wow! Only an hour! Maybe I'll get this done yet today!

The e-mail directed that I open an attachment. It, too, was a form. I examined it. There stood a field, "PROBLEM RESOLUTION." I moved the mouse pointer to it and clicked. The pop-up said that the problem was entered and is now under consideration.

To that time I had spent half an afternoon attempting a simple change in our health care plan. I had made progress. About two steps forward, with a hundred to go.

Aren't modern computers wonderful? These forms are concocted by *systems analysts*, and I've had many previous runs-in with these chaps earlier in life. Usually they are rather competent. But in developing a new application, such as this form, they sometimes forget a little piece of computer coding, and the whole thing fails. They rely on user feedback, such as mine, to highlight the problem so they can resolve it. Why in the world they could not have asked some of their office help to fill in *beta* versions of the form before releasing it as a plague on the general public baffles me. Just lazy, I guess. Or incompetent.

HEADACHE

Roy, a close friend, colleague, and fellow grad school student, was working toward a doctorate in Chemistry. We shared many good and trying times, conducting study in the field of *Radiochemistry*, employing radioactive isotopes in chemistry. At times this helps track where a given product winds up in the aftermath of a reaction. At other times it studies natural radioactivity, as in radiocarbon dating.

Goodly supplies of various materials supported our research. We used lead bricks by the many tons, stacked up to make a sort of doghouse, inside of which our very sensitive gamma ray spectrometers were placed. Metallic lead shields the gamma detectors from cosmic rays, lowers the radioactive *background*, thus increasing sensitivity. A second heavily-used commodity was mercury. Placed in a steel pipe, it, too, as a heavy metal, would attenuate the background.

Of course many other items and chemicals were needed. And one day Roy, thumbing through a J. T. Baker catalog, happened across something that caught his attention: "Aspirin – 325 mg tablets – 10,000 count." Now who but a hospital needed ten thousand aspirin tablets? The thought itself touched Roy's humorous side. But the price! Why, the little devils in that quantity were a handful to the penny. So Roy added it to his list.

A week or so later it arrived – a large, brown bottle, about the size of a gallon pickle jar, the J. T. Baker label prominently thereupon, with a large screw-on plastic lid covering an opening easily admitting a person's hand. Inside rested the ten thousand little pills. He set this on the corner of his desk, and at the staff meeting that week announced, in a jocular mood, their presence. He added: "Should anyone ever need an aspirin, stop by my desk and help yourself. I have enough to get through grad school and then some."

This invitation spread through our group, and then through the department. The bottle was empty in less than a year!

We could not believe it! The staff had consumed ten thousand aspirin tablets in about ten months! Roy placed a reorder.

Now there's a further story about my dear friend. If I recall correctly, he was the youngest of the seven sons of a prominent surgeon and physician. His six siblings had achieved success as doctors, lawyers, or other professionals, and Roy was in the spotlight, so to speak, feeling enormous pressure and the need to succeed. Grad school is hard enough. Lord, I know: I survived it as well. But through thick and thin we stuck it out, and I was joyously happy to be at Roy's graduation, shake his hand, say, "Well done, Doctor Roy!"

As an undergraduate he had been an ROTC student, and needed yet to complete his two year's commitment on active duty. He served in the Army Reserves the several years spent in graduate studies, so had advanced from Second Lieutenant to First Lieutenant, and, with the doctorate conferred, to Captain. Now, schooling complete, he was required to report to active duty. So off he went, a doctorate in radiochemistry, to a military post.

Just where do you think the Army would place such an individual? Perhaps something to do with CBR [3] warfare? Perhaps a nuclear weapons programs? No. He was placed on the staff as a radiologist at an Army hospital.

So how about his father and siblings? Did Roy live up to expectations? People would ask, "And what happened to Roy?"

The Answer: "He's on the staff at Walter Reed." Indeed, and so he was! Amazing – Roy's years-long anxiety and headache had now become passé.

Yes, there is a God. And at times He looks at those who have been struggling hard, trusting in Him, and metes out an interesting reward. And I thank Him for having so lovingly provided for my dear friend and colleague.

---

[3] Chemical, Biological or Radiological

LACIE

A typical workday: I sat at my desk, various reports ready for review, signature, forwarding or archiving, resting in my *IN* box, accompanying drafts of the yet-to-be-finished. An assortment of reference manuals and books sat within easy reach, including a large red tome: the dictionary. This essential tool supported conduct of edits to the drafts and reports. *IN* also contained arriving mail, magazines, and other such matter.

Phone interruptions were common and at times welcomed. They provided a break from monotony, and often posed interesting questions and challenges, or at other times a bit of friendly intercollegiate exchange. From my small office I assisted the laboratory chief in management of daily operations, affairs, and workflow. I was his deputy.

The desk intercom barked occasionally with statements such as, "Mr. T – air conditioning unit #2 is down again." "Mr. T – there's a stoppage in the ladies' restroom." "Mr. T – visitors have arrived in the lobby." And on it went, my responding to various mini-emergencies as they were announced, handling not only flow of technical work and reports, but keeping the ship sailing, so to speak, on a relatively even keel.

Now, my first foray into management had been as a new officer in the Army. I retain the primary rule therefrom in my mind at all times: "A manager is responsible for two things: accomplishment of the mission, and the care of h/er/is troops." To that end on returning from lunch I once observed the "Good Humor" truck drive by our small campus.

I turned my auto about, followed it, and at its next stop approached the driver. I asked that, on his daily rounds, he drive into our compound with his music going, and park at a breezeway off the rear of the building. Thereafter he did so. It gave me pleasure to announce over the PA system, "Good Humor truck has arrived. Fifteen minute break authorized." And staff appreciation was evident.

There were interpersonal squabbles to handle as well. "Test equipment needed in the TV Lab was borrowed by Experimental Group and need be returned or work will stop" … "Experimental Group will have a work stoppage without the test equipment." And one item in particular seemed to occur, as regular as clockwork, or perhaps calendar work.

Every fourth Monday a Ms. Lacie would appear at my doorway: "Mr. T! We have a problem in the typing pool!" These interpersonals required immediate attention, the leaving of my desk, and the going forth to spread oil on troubled waters.

Ahh, yes – the daily life and routine of a midlevel manager …

Then a rather interesting turn of events did so turn. Our top Executive, director of the whole agency, was a political appointee and served at the pleasure of the President. And when President Jimmy "Peanuts" Carter came to office, our then-Executive met with displeasure and was discharged, to be replaced by a bright, new appointee, formerly an assistant to a congressman. This forebode ill.

The new director came with a plan: the entire agency was full of bureaucratic deadwood, in need of replacement, top to bottom. A bloodbath washed over us. All but one of the very top office-holders, the Bureau Chiefs, were "retired." My wife and I found ourselves at a retirement dinner two, three times per month, as the purge continued down the chain of command.

The new director took an interesting misstep his very first week on the job. Our working hours had been 0800 to 1645 daily. He changed it to 0900 to 1745, a one-hour delay. This was a decree. There was no consulting the existing employee-management board, no polling of employees, nil. Just a flat proclamation.

In quite short order representatives of the National Treasury Employees Union appeared in front of the building, and in the public access ways. They were soliciting signatures on a petition to unionize the agency! Since its inception in 1934 it had been a non-union shop, despite several attempts over the years by a union. Only one such succeeded. This one.

We became a union shop!

Well! A rather abrupt change in the situation came about, and particularly in organization. All managers were required to attend a sequence of briefings on what this entailed. We were no longer allowed to directly interact with an employee outside of union-negotiated rules. And the union rules had to be drawn up, agreed to by union and management, and posted for all to read when and if desired. Naturally management had a lot of reading and re-training to do, and I was so conscripted.

I greeted this shift in employee-management with some trepidation. How am I to continue my daily routine? What new requirements will be added to my chores?

And then a wonderful thing happened. A "fourth Monday" occurred, heralded as usual by Ms. Lacie's appearance at my door. She began her usual announcement of problems in the typing pool, in her monthly, characteristically very unflattering, tones bespeaking anger. I interrupted. I bade her simply put her expression of concern on "hold," picked up the desk phone, and punched the PA system button. I spoke:

"Shop Steward. Mr. T's Office. Now!"

Dutifully did the union representative appear. I addressed the steward and said, "Ms. Lacie has a problem. Please escort her to the cafeteria area, discuss the issue, prepare a plan for its amelioration and present it to me. Do so in a reasonable time." Therewith the duo was dismissed.

I sat back in my chair, mused a bit:

"Hey! This union shop thing ain't so bad after all!"

MOUSES

When our girls were quite young, wife and I would read children's stories to them, and encourage them to read from the books as well. And to this day, my younger daughter, now an engineer for the Navy, remembers one about some churchmice, and asked if I would include it in my short essays. This is that story. It is not my original, but I know not its first author. Although it appears in myriad forms on the internet, per her request I re-tell it here as best I can, in my own style.

* * * * *

Once upon a time there was a cat who lived in a country church. She was a *mouser*, a cat people kept to keep the mice at bay, lest they overrun everything. The cat and the mice maintained a balance.

The church was ancient, drafty, and very cold in the winter. Tho she had an old but comfortable blanket in a large wicker basket as a bed, poor cat was always cold, sometimes very, very cold, in winter. The minister and lay persons looked after her, grooming her sometimes, making sure she had enough food and water, and on Sundays gave her some milk to drink..

Cat liked living in the church, even though she was sometimes very cold. She did her job well, chasing the mice away, keeping the church from becoming infested, and welcoming anyone who came in. After all, there were few visitors except on Sunday.

During the week she saw just the minister or his wife who brought her food and water, cleaned her litter box, and the lady who came to clean the church one day a week. But she was happy, knowing that she was serving God, and that God loved her.

The church was not without mice. If it were, cat would be out of a job! Cat chased the mice. The mice ran. Cat ran after them. This cat and mouse game happened every day, the mice scurrying off as cat ran after them.

Over cat's lifetime, some of the mice died. One day four of them did. Being churchmice, they went to Saint Peter, keeper of the pearly gates. He said, "Well – what have we here? Four little mice. Why are you here, and what do you want?"

They said, "We are four poor churchmice who lived all our lives in God's house, and now that we are dead, we didn't know where else to go except to come to God."

Saint Peter said, "Well, then, let me check my books ... Yes, here it is. You *are* churchmice, and good ones, too. God wants you to be in heaven with Him, and all the churchmice before you. How can I make your time here pleasant?"

The mice thought a bit, and talked among themselves. Then one of them said, "All our lives we had to run from the church cat. She chased us everywhere, and would not let us get into a lot of the church stuff. We are very tired of running. Could you do something about that?"

Saint Peter thought for just a bit, and said, "That's exactly what all the churchmice said. I'll give you the same as I gave them." He

Michael Toia

then waved his hand above and across the mice. And magically, *roller skates* appeared on their feet! The mice looked, and were delighted! They thanked Saint Peter. He opened the gates. The mice skated into heaven.

A while later Saint Peter saw the mice skating along. He asked, "Are you happy? Is there anything else you need?"

They said, "Oh, no. Heaven is so wonderful, and so beautiful. And God smiles and waves at us when we skate nearby. So do Jesus, Moses, and the whole gang. And the best part is these wonderful, magical roller skates. Thank you so much!" And off they skated.

Well, some years later cat got very old. The day came that she, too, died. The minister, his wife and lay leaders had a small, wonderful little service for her and they buried her in the church graveyard.

Cat, having lived all her life in church, did as the mice had done. She looked to be close to God. And this brought her to Saint Peter, who said, "Well – what have we here ? A cat? Why are you here, and what do you want?"

Cat said, "I am a poor church cat who lived all my life in God's house, and now that I am dead, I didn't know where else to go except to get closer to God."

Saint Peter said, "Well, then, let me check my books ... Yes, here it is. You *are* a church cat, and a good one too. God wants you to be in heaven with Him. How can I make your time here pleasant?"

Cat said, "All my life I lived in a church, and had to chase away mice. I worked very hard at it, but grew old. And at times I was cold: very, very cold. I am very tired. I would like just a nice, comfortable, warm place to curl up and rest. Could you do something about that?"

Saint Peter thought for a minute, then waved his hand above and across cat. And magically, a soft, pink, warm cloudlet appeared next to cat, who stepped aboard it, and laid down on it. The feeling was wonderful. Cat thanked Saint Peter very much. Saint Peter opened the gates. The cloudlet wafted cat into heaven.

A while later Saint Peter saw cat enjoying her nice, little pink cloudlet. He asked, "Are you happy? Is there anything else you need?"

Cat said, "Oh, no. Heaven is so wonderful, and so beautiful. And God smiles and waves at me every time I drift by. So do Jesus, Moses, and the whole gang. But the best part of heaven is the *meals on wheels*."

PRO KEN

The day started pleasantly, good weather, comfortable temperature and humidity, not an oddity for Georgia but on the less probable side. We half dozen sat at our desks, going over blueprints, planning new modifications to the flying stock. Our mission was to retrofit aircraft, to endow them with new capabilities. Warren and I worked communications and navigation; our office mates, nap-of-the-earth night flight, and assorted other aircraft systems.

Mid morning, the chief exited his office, a bit disturbed, came to Ken's desk carrying the draft of a field test report, and somewhat exasperatedly said:

"Ken! I've read this report several times. I can't decipher what it says! You wrote it! Do a rewrite! Make it clear who went where, what happened, and results of the trip." Ken opined that everything was already written down, as clear as day, as well as he could make it. The chief turned about, brushed past my desk, looked at me, and tossed the report practically into my lap, saying:

"Mike! Read this thing. Maybe it's just me. See if it makes sense to you, and let me know, today, before noon." He strode back to his office. With that, other duties, drawings and reports set aside for a bit, I took up Ken's report, and began to read.

It was a bit mystifying. I turned about, faced Ken's desk, and began asking what *this* and *that* and the other things meant. As questioning continued, he filled me in with more details. *Who* went on the trip? Ken provided names. *Where* did they go? Ken provided details. *Why* did the go? *When, where, how?* I re-read the report and still could not piece it all together.

I went to the chief's office, entered, and said, "Sorry, chief. I read this report several times. I talked to Ken. I still can't quite piece it all together, or for that matter, piece together most of it." He replied, "Sit down with Ken. See if you can re-write it so it makes sense. We can't use it as it stands."

Orders are orders. I left the chief's office, went to my desk, sat down, scratched my head and tried reading the report one more time. Additional concepts had gelled: get the answers to *who, when, where, why, what* and *how*. Then it dawned on me. The report contained practically no nouns! Mostly pronouns! So with a highlighter, I marked each and every one of those non-specific little demonic placeholders.

After so doing, I spun around again, faced Ken, told him what the chief asked me to do, and said, "Let's get this thing done." Pointing to my first highlight, I said, "Here you said *we* went on this trip. *Who* "we?"

Ken answered, "You know – Gordon, Roger, Dave." I continued: "Did *you* go as well?" He said, of course. So I took notes: for the pronoun *who* I inserted instead the list of names. Then I asked, "*Where* did all of you go?" Again Ken said, "You know – down to Eglin Air Force Base." So I took a note, replaced the *where* with the actual noun designating the place. We continued in like manner. In a way Ken was probably driven a bit nuts about the procedure, but I insisted: there shall be no pronouns in this report. None. Zilch. Nada.

After taking all the notes, I turned back to my desk, took the original report with scribbles all over it, and its good helping of *post-its* stuck here and there. I began a re-write. After the first, I examined it in more detail, found a few pronouns that had yet escaped scrutiny, turned to Ken, and obtained their designated nouns. A second re-write resulted, and I sat, read over the report. It now seemed to make sense. Good sense.

I gave it to Ken, and asked him to read it. He did. We made a few corrections, and a final re-write resulted, was read by both of us, and Ken said, "Yeah, this is right. It's what I said in the first place. What's the chief's problem?"

I took the new version to the chief's office, put it in his *IN* basket, and went to lunch. After, the chief came to Ken and said, "Hey! This makes sense. It's a good report. Why didn't you say so in the first place?" Ken opined that, in fact, he had! The chief turned to me, said a "thanks," and asked what the difference was. I said, "Read the first report, then look at the rewrite. The second one has no pronouns. None at all. There's the difference."

That day, Ken and I, friends before the episode, remained so, but he took on a new nickname: *Pro*Ken – for his love of pronouns.

Further, that day I somehow became the office's unofficial technical editor, a skill I had never tried to hone and to this day am a bit baffled as to how it developed.

RATTLER

L ife in the Southeast can be quite comfortable, enjoyable, after one's becoming accustomed to the climate. The outdoorsman finds a good deal of solace in fishing and hunting, alligator wrestling, worm snoring, and many similar endeavors. Although born Yankees, wife and I settled into the area nicely, living alternately in Georgia and the Florida panhandle.

Not an avid hunter, I nonetheless spent much of my youth outdoors, among the deer, rabbits, raccoons, and so many other creatures of the wild. More than one fall season, walking across a field of tall grass, did my approach disturb a nesting pheasant that took noisily to its wing. It was always a surprise as the bird so completely blends into its surroundings: it's invisible on the ground.

And far more dramatic, on coming across a quail's nest, the bird seems literally to explode from between the feet, as if a half-dozen cherry-bomb firecrackers had been tossed on the shoes. That unexpected, sudden and *booming* event causes the heart to skip several beats before resumption, the restoration of breathing, and reasonable recovery.

A Dothan, Alabama TV channel provided coverage to the Gulf. Sunday afternoons it aired the *Red Hollander* show, an hour devoted to the outdoor enthusiast. Red characteristically hosted various sportsmen who talked about their particular love and experiences.

One guest was a fella, a "Good Ole Boy" from Southwest Georgia, just a bit East of Dothan. He was a rattlesnake hunter. Red and he got into just how it is that one hunts for such. I listened, with piqued interest, as our farm, our homestead at the time, abounded in the like, and I believed what was to be taught could offer guidance as to their avoidance, or at least to be more cognizant of their existence.

The show continued. The Good Ole Boy explained that rattlers don't make burrows themselves, but move into former quarters of other small animals that had. He and his brother generally hunted together. His instructions:

* * * * *

"We walks along, through the woods an' fields, on a warm day, lookin' fer a rattler out sunnin' hisself. Ole animal burrows are ideal spots, small mud areas with no vegetation, sittin' exposed in the sunlight. We approach, real careful-like. Most of the time there ain't no snake.

"We carries a hunk o' half-inch water pipe along, an' a flask. Ginger-like, slow, we pokes the pipe down the hole, listenin' to the other end. Thet annoys a snake, an' he'll sound off, shakin' his rattle. Ya can hear it through the pipe. Then we know we got one.

"When there ain't a sound – thet usually happens – we takes the flask … it's got gasoline in it … pours a wee bit into the end of the pipe, cups a hand o'er the end, an' blow gently, waftin' them gas fumes into the burrow. If there's a rattler in there, he's comin' right out!"

The audience – myself and others in TV land – listened. The Ole Boy showed some photos of several of their finds, showed off a few snake skins, a belt and a wallet made of other skins, and photos of their hunting forays. It was engaging and interesting, drinking in the local culture, enjoying the Ole Boy's style, admiring his "intestinal fortitude," his technique. and the whole procedure. Then Red asked,

"What's the worst fright you ever got doin' this kinda huntin'?"

His response:

"Well, one day brother an' me come upon a small crik bank, lots o sand, mud, clay, an' there wuz a large burrow. We crept up on it real careful-like, lookin' for what we was after: a big rattler. There weren't any.

"I took my piece o' pipe, started it careful-like down that hole, listenin' to the end, hopin' to hear that tell-tale sound. There was nuthin'.

"Once that pipe got down the hole as far is it could, an' it was a deep one, I got my flask, poured a bit o' gas into the pipe, put the flask back in ma pocket – ya gotta be ready to act real quick-like. You're always expectin' this time your gonna find the granddaddy of all them other rattlers ya ever done found before.

"I cupped my hand over the end of the pipe, took a deep breath, ready to waft them gas fumes down the hole ...

"An' jest then come outta that hole a quail, explodin' outta there, right almost into ma face! Scared the bejeebers outta me. Outta ma brother, too!"

* * * * *

Red howled with laughter. I howled – so much I fell out of my chair, to the floor. Then Red asked, "What did ya do next?"

The Good Ole Boy stroked his hair, thought a bit, then said, "Gave up snake huntin' for six months."

THE CELL

T he cell phone began in the late 1970's. Motorola invented the system, installed two cell towers in the Washington, DC area, and by exhibit, demonstrated how such a system could work. The first phones were about half the size of a brick, and had the heft and weight of the whole thing, plus. Thankfully technology advanced rapidly afterwards.

Our daughters came to their teen years. Several companies offered cell service. Each lass in turn acquired her very own phone, small, purse-sized, easily carried about. And younger daughter, excited about her first such, read its manual intently, to see what it offered and how to get the most of it.

In the instructions was a note about assurance of long battery life: use the phone to run the battery down, almost completely discharged. Charge it fully. Do the same again. This is akin to breaking in the engine of a new car: drive in a specific manner for the first two hundred fifty miles, then change oil from the original "break in" formulation to the standard stuff.

Daughter took the instructions intently to heart. The manual showed the additional features on the device, such as a calendar, calculator, and a few games.

Ahh, yes – games! She found one that caught her interest. And the very next day, during a family road trip to our little cabin in the mountains, well out of the service area, the long drive afforded an excellent spell of a few hours to while away time with it. Her sister, riding along, assisted and advised, the two of them becoming fairly well engaged in the game. On and off over the weekend she continued, watching the battery charge condition, playing the game rather often, in the lulls of otherwise family time.

We enjoyed a family weekend outdoors, visited a small local waterfall at the end of a beautiful trail though several hundred feet of mountain laurel, beneath tall hemlock trees, over a thick, spongy blanket of needles fallen decades past, to a small bluff of heavily moss-covered limestone. The falls was known to the locals but not to tourists. It was a quiet, beautiful, secluded spot, beneath which the stream ponded into an area about the size of a backyard swimming pool. Several times before had we visited and splashed about in that cold, mountain water, not quite deep enough for swimming, just knee depth.

The weekend evenings passed with a bit of time viewing a small, black-and-white television set offering its very best, a poor picture with snow, interference, and fluttering. Satellite TV broadcast was yet on the inventors' drawing boards. We warmed ourselves by the fireplace, popped corn, some of which burst into flame. Consigning the incinerated pieces back to the fire, we enjoyed the remainder. And we had a habit of assembling jigsaw puzzles on the large living room floor, a nice family get-together and a means to relax, let the time slip away.

Overnight all slept well. A tiny brook babbled by, its song lulling one to dreamland quite quickly. But the weekend all too soon came to an end. It was time to repack the overnight bags and do the drive home. The girls sat in the back, once again engaging in another run at that cell phone game.

All the while one heard beeps, bloops, squoogles, and other game-related cacophony issuing forth from the device. Wife and I enjoyed the mountain scenery as we had so often done over the past quarter century of traversing this route. We had our own pet names for selected rock formations, road junctions, and barns along the way.

Across the Laurel Highlands we drove, across the Eastern Divide, down the seven mile descent from Allegheny Mountain, through Cumberland, along the Potomac to Paw Paw. From thence we took again to mountain roads leading to Winchester, VA. We continued, coming at last within cell phone range of our home to the East.

The racket of the phone was heard the entire trip. And as we exited Winchester, it began a new system of squawks. Daughter must have reached a new level of game play, one to which she had not previously ascended. Even she was puzzled. No action of hers could influence that sequence of sounds. She emoted: "What did I do? What's happening?"

Sister solved her problem:

"It's a phone. It's ringing."

VENISON

D eep suburban living, on the edge of that cusp giving way to farms, horses, and cattle, is our chosen way of life. Although commuting to work, doctors, shopping, theater and such takes considerable time otherwise well-spent, to us the rewards are worth it. A few acres of lawn was presided over by our home which rests on a little rise at the end of our street, the rise affording a beautiful view of a near-rural vista. To the West a herd of magnificent stallions and mares prances about on a horse farm, and beautiful sunsets usher in the night.

Now, I have always enjoyed gardening. There is something quite relaxing about spending time tilling the soil, tending a small patch of tomatoes, peppers, lettuce and more, that drags the mind and soul completely out of the workplace, offers good exercise, and later induces a good night's sleep. My activity includes the tending of a small orchard, a few apple, peach, and cherry trees. But the whole enterprise comes with a price, a deer price – yes – deer. Hungry deer. A small herd roam the area and consume almost any bit of vegetation rising from the ground in an attempt at life. It's quite a problem.

Hunting to thin the herd is generally permitted at certain times of the year. But the nature of our area, the density of homes, renders gun hunting too dangerous. A neighbor, however, is a bow hunter and, by mutual consent, will hunt the local properties, ours included. I simply ask that he inform us by hailing or telephone when he is active, that we can be aware and not become accidental prey. The arrangement has worked well for many a year.

A defense against deer is fencing, though the critters can easily leap across rather high ones. A similar product is a lightweight material, *deer netting*. It's somewhat like chicken wire, made of tough, thin, black plastic wire-like material. Wrapped loosely about the trunk or branches of a small tree apparently frustrates the deer's ability to access and strip the bark and branchlets therefrom.

The third defense is the use of a repellent spray product. I find it effective, its having attenuated deer damage to our fruit trees. These sprays are sold in local hardware and home supply centers. A Saturday morning found me at one such, a goodly clientele roaming about, and several standing on line awaiting a turn at the checkout counter. The line moved along. In a bit I was second, a pleasant woman ahead. She had brought forth a container of deer spray, asked the counterman if it might work, as the deer considered her extensive and beautiful flower garden a salad bar – so she explained.

Now, why would the counterman know? Recall the scene: we were in a rural hardware store, and the establishment's employees advise on *everything* available for sale – nuts, bolts, pipe fittings, drain products, paint, fertilizer – everything in the store. And we, their customers, rely on that advice. It's most often right on the mark as we purchase the doohickies and thingamabobs so necessary to patch our homes back into working order.

The woman was asking about the product, concerned that a quart of the stuff had a price tag of a bit over twenty dollars. She inquired: was there not another such, less expensive? The counterman explained that, yes, there was, in fact there were several, but in their experience not really very effective. This product had the best success at deer deterrent, and that is why it's the only brand the small store stocks.

She hesitated, thought, then said she would consider it, ask advice of her gardening club, not purchase it right then but would return in a day or so. She left the container on the counter, turned, was about to leave, but in the crowd came face to face with me, unable to proceed until I myself jostled aside a bit to expedite here passage. And in that time we had a brief conversation, actually one sided, as I said:

"My neighbor is a bow hunter, and I'm sure he'd be happy to be of assistance. I can give you his phone number if you like."

She looked at me, a shocked look, that said it all: how could I *conceive* of harming those beautiful, graceful creatures? She said nothing. She needed not. Her body language and facial expression did all. Then I added,

"There's a book store in the bit of a mall down the road a tad. They have a nice one on venison recipes."

That did it! She continued her reticence, gave me the look that could drop a speeding buffalo in its tracks, edged past, glanced back with great disgust, and exited the store. I was simply trying to be of assistance, but instead stood there, having by the process developed horns, a long, forked tail, a deep red complexion, holding a six-foot, red trident – Satan in person! Ahhh well – I try. There's no pleasing some people.

ANNAMARIE'S

T ourism is Florida's largest industry, and the next largest surprises many. It's not citrus. The center of that is a band across the middle of the state, from the ocean on the east to the gulf on the west. Tourism, aside from a hot spot in the Orlando area, hugs the coast as if a rind about the state. The innards, the state's main body, stretching from Mobile / Pensacola in the northwest to the Okefenokee, shared with Georgia, and on down to the Everglades, supports cattle ranching, the state's second largest industry.

The Capes Canaveral / Kennedy areas were two small spots catering to rocket and satellite launching. They supported quite an industry, with contractors and government persons constantly coming and going throughout the year, until the administration shut down the space shuttle program. But rocket launching continues quite a bit from the Cape Canaveral sites along the ocean. This activity yet brings many a contractor in support of the processes.

Business often took us to the area as contractors, working on various satellite-related systems over the years. A few occasions found a confluence of two related contracts, with teams from both on location simultaneously. My boss, Bob, was the government contracting officer's technical representative, the COTR, of one, and the spouse of Shirley, COTR of the other. They planned their frequent contract reviews to be in each others' company while away from home.

We had developed a custom of staying at one or two particular beachside hotels south of Cocoa and Patrick. Our choice was influenced by availability of government-rate rooms offered at the contract-allowed per diem rate. Higher rates required augmentation from one's personal wallet. Lodging closer to the center of activity commanded those higher rates because of their convenience, hence the drift some few tens of miles from the Canaveral and Kennedy launch centers.

The area became as a second home. Significant portions of our life were spent there. We became familiar with the many dining possibilities, shopping areas, wash-n-fold laundry and dry cleaners, and establishments of all sorts. After a day's work we'd occasionally gather as a sort of extended family out for a leisurely evening meal and conversation, sometimes about the projects' conditions, problems, resolutions, and so forth, other times centered about sports, team standings, or just general chatter without any specific goal other than to enjoy one another's company.

There were spates of activity involving shift work, and a need to strike out individually to seek nourishment. The area was a tourist Mecca offering many fine restaurants. A handful were on our commonly visited list, but necessity sometimes demanded a foray to an unfamiliar establishment. Other times, when work offered a lull and a bit of time off, we would strike out individually to find something new. In the latter mode I came across a dining experience at a then-recently-opened restaurant, Annamarie's, and settled in for an evening meal.

The fare was Cajun, a style I had come to appreciate during a previous episode of life as a resident of the Florida Panhandle. Our home had been well west of Tallahassee, near the gulf coast and not far East of Louisiana. Cajun establishments abounded there. Many were quite good, a few excellent. But that evening I observed: none could beat Annamarie's. It was the finest I had eaten. I made note of it, and revisited from time to time, sometimes alone, sometimes with one or two other team members.

An evening came. We gathered in the hotel lobby, divided into a few small groups. One wanted to visit a particular restaurant. Another chose a different dining experience.

Shirley looked at me, said, "Mike, you haven't recommended a restaurant in quite a while. Do you have a good suggestion?" I thought, then said, "Do you like Cajun?" She said she *loved* it. So Annamarie's it was to be. We filed into two rental cars, six in ours, I in the back seat, Bob at the controls, Shirley seated beside him. Bob drove off. I gave directions.

Over the bit of chatter and conversation Bob announced, "Mike, this had better be good. Shirley and I lived just outside New Orleans some time back, and she considers herself the best Cajun cook in the world." Shirley emphatically punctuated his statement. The other three in the car joined in: This had better be good – or else! "Good Lord!" I thought. "What had I gotten myself into? I may be in deep trouble here."

We rode. Down along A1A, the beachside highway, to a causeway about a half score miles distant, over the river to the mainland and into a small, old-line Florida city, and along its main street. And there it stood: Annamarie's. Bob parked. We extricated our body parts from the cramped interior, made it to the front door and entered. The maître'd greeted us, took a nose count, and ushered us to a few tables.

I could continue. My mind was nervously occupied with Shirley's reaction to the anticipated evening experience and the fare. We dined. We chatted. Everyone had a relaxing good time of it, perhaps myself the exception, with my Bob-induced preoccupation. But the meal was, to me, as excellent as was the ambiance and company at hand. At least not all would be lost.

We continued, finished the last of the establishment's offerings, then began the return trip, reinserted ourselves into the sedan. Bob pulled from the parking spot, chatting about the evening and that Annamarie's was, in fact, a fine choice that all seemed to enjoy. And then he turned to Shirley, asked teasingly and provocatively, "Well, hon, was it better than yours?" Shirley answered: "No."

"But it was as good!"

Bob congratulated me, saying it isn't often someone can achieve that state with her. Shirley agreed, thanked me. I breathed a deep sigh of relief.

COCKTAIL

There I stood, in unfamiliar surroundings, a young, awkward and inept, geek-like professional engineer, lacking social graces, immersed in a cocktail party. Told this is part of "networking," the building of contacts, lists of colleagues, and access to fonts of information, I had attended. It seemed at that point in my upbringing something necessary, another step in ascension to adulthood, all the more unwelcome as I do not imbibe.

Others tried to make small talk, welcomed me as a relatively new associate. I tried to reciprocate, clumsily, nervously, with perhaps a modicum of success. And as the evening wore on, it developed that certain fellow partiers were pleasant, and others somewhat less so.

Small talk. About what? Almost invariably questions about what one does for a living and where. Well, I've worked for the government for quite a spell, and at that time, for the Federal Communications Commission – the FCC. Early on I discovered that, offering this as an answer, led to a bit of uncomfortable discussion, such as, "My TV gets a lot of interference. Can you do something about that, or tell me who I can call?" In answer to such inquiry, there generally isn't. But the inquiring party, after a few martinis or so, will often not drop the subject but continue in still more annoying tones. I wish I could offer good advice, but with such general and vague questions none exists.

A protective move for these situations is necessary. When asked what I do for a living, I reply cordially, "I work for the government." This oft catalyzes a follow-up: "Oh! What do you do?" The honest reply is that I work for one of those three-letter agencies.

Now things get interesting. The inquisitive one will not take the cue that I would prefer not to discuss the matter, but becomes piqued: *which* agency? CIA? NSA? FBI? And on it goes. All attempts to brush off the question and change the subject falls in the Vogon [4] category: "Resistance is Useless."

I came up with a marvelous defense that can be erected at this time. After repeating several times that I'd rather not say, the inquisition continuing unabated and intensifying, I take the inquirer into deepest confidence, and in hushed tones, say that it is a secret that must be kept, lest the others learn of it and shun me. I weave a bit of a tale: "My job requires secrecy. If others knew of it, my mission would be seriously compromised."

"I work for the IRS. I'm an undercover field auditor."

That does the trick. I thereby don a cloak of leprosy. The inquirer fades away, and by evening's end no one wishes to speak to me. Just as well, as I have found the cocktail hour to be one of the least pleasant endeavors for passing an evening. And I am rarely invited to others.

---

[4] D. Adams, *Hitchhiker's Guide to the Galaxy* – Vogons are extremely dull, mentally slow, and officious far beyond a fault.

Michael Toia

ENGLISH

E nglish? Ugh! It was a required course throughout school, from first grade to college, the one I disliked the most, with the possible exception of history. As to the latter: I see no reason to study it. Simply catch the rerun. But let's here return to the story line.

The study of English, or for that matter the language of one's birth country, is important, to be sure. Without it, our communication would be reduced to a system of grunts, howls, pointing fingers, shoulder shrugs, strange dance moves and so. It's vital that one have facility of expression. It's rewarding to have a good command of that facility. That command leads to an amazing world of ersatz travel, wonderful imagination, fantasy, and even reality and understanding.

Yes, I rather disliked English. But quite early in life, even before first grade, I found a love of reading. Relatives presented me with age-appropriate books on special occasions, such as Christmas, birthdays. I devoured them. They told fantastic stories, tales of instruction, and facts of the world, things about flying reindeer, witches in gingerbread houses, princesses and princes.

Our grade school, small though it was, had a library of about two hundred seventy titles. In an assigned third grade reading session, teacher said we were to pick a book and begin reading it. I did not do so. Teacher asked why. It was simple: I had already read all two hundred seventy or so books. She tested me, pulled a few at random from the shelves, asked me what each was about, and I knew: I passed her test.

That fascination, the reading of books, then magazines, newspapers, journal articles, etc. continued until I reached age forty. Those readings taught me ninety percent of what I know, and contain almost all of what I do not know, in a form that can be consulted as needed.

At forty I found the drive to read waned. And for a reason. An eye exam disclosed that my vision had faded. Reading glasses were needed. The doctor, after an examination, asked, "When you try to read, you find your arms too short?" suggesting perhaps I could not focus on reading material at normal distances.

My answer: I'm a maintenance engineer for electronic systems. Equipment rooms are large enough for the equipment, but not generous on maintenance space. On trying to read the various meters, I discovered I could not back off far enough: a wall arrested my progress. A small magnifying glass added to my toolkit was needed to read the meters correctly. He chuckled, then annotated his examination report. I inquired: what was he writing? "You're the first to tell me the room was too small!" But it was.

In the course of doing that reading, from age four on, there developed a means of verbal and written expression, a vocabulary, a knowledge of how and where to research and dig out facts, meanings, data and such on demand.

On graduating college with a degree in Physics I was offered, and accepted, a position in a large research laboratory as a junior scientist/engineer. The laboratory ran a program in which all newly hired technical personnel reported to the cafeteria at 9 AM each Friday morning. It was an in-house, mandatory training program. About forty of us did so for the session I was assigned to attend.

The instructor handed out information, data sheets of measurements, a sketch of a laboratory setup and a list of all equipment used to obtain the data. His instruction: in the next two hours write a technical report detailing what had happened, why the measurements were taken, a statement of the problem dictating the need of the scientific investigation, the findings and conclusion, and their implications.

We studied the material. We were ordered to work as individuals on the assignment. We wrote. We composed our individual reports. We did so until 10:50 AM. Instructor gave a ten minute warning, and at eleven commanded "Pencils down! Turn in your papers. Exit the area and return to your assigned work station." So we did.

The following Friday came. Instructor called the class to order, called six names, commanded the six to come forward. He handed each his respective report prepared the week earlier. Each had a letter grade upon it: "A." He said, "Congratulations. You have passed the final exam for this course. Report back to your normal work area. Tell your supervisor you have been released from this class. You are qualified technical writers." We six were dismissed.

It surprised us. It surprised me, one of the half dozen.

Me? A *writer*? Where did *that* come from?

FAIRHAVEN

One beautiful September evening she accepted my proposal and we became engaged, with a date set just a few months in the future, before the Army would call for fulfillment of a commitment previously made. Four hundred miles separated us. It became my task to select our first household, and in short order it was so. A small cottage on the property of, and behind a large home, was advertised for rent, a lease signed. It was set in a nice grove of mature trees, in a beautiful, small, old-line village near the central New Jersey shore. I carried my bride across its threshold that winter.

The structure consisted of one living room, approximately sixteen feet on a side, one bedroom about ten by twelve feet, connected by a somewhat narrow passageway containing a pullman-style kitchen. A single bathroom located adjacent to the bedroom was inline with the kitchen. Completing the structure was a utility room yet farther behind the bath, accessible from the bedroom. The overall floor plan was a U-shape, wrapped about a very mature maple tree.

There was no air conditioning. Not many homes had such in that day, and the location with Ocean breezes would largely ameliorate the need of same. There was also no central furnace in the house! Each of its rooms had its own means to obtain heat.

In the living room stood a kerosene stove toward the rear wall, a brown metal structure a bit larger than an average washing machine. It was fed via a copper tube from a fifty-five gallon drum resting on a stand behind the house. The wall opposite the kitchen entranceway was prominently dominated by a large, beautiful, wood-burning fireplace, a so-named *Heat-0-Lator*. A wood fire warmed a metal firebox, and air entering vents on both sides at hearth level passed behind, warmed, and rose to exit vents above, spreading nicely throughout the room. It did a wonderful job.

A hurricane had come by the shore the previous fall and ravaged the beaches and boardwalks. Many trees had been damaged or destroyed. Their tangled remains were piled high in various community lots. We purchased a bow saw, one containing a band-type blade three feet long and an inch wide, four teeth to the inch, designed to cut trees. It provided a good deal of exercise evenings and weekends. The effort kept us in firewood the entire winter.

I became rather skilled keeping that fireplace well stoked. But I knew little of the various types of wood found in the lots. Some trees attracted many people, others were hardly, or not at all, attended to. The latter I approached and worked as there was little competition for their wood. Many fine fireplace logs were cut therefrom. But we later discovered they were very difficult to split.

The cottage came with a sledge and five steel splitting wedges. Two could be put into service to try to extricate a third from a log, although this was sometimes difficult. And one large log swallowed all five of the wedges without yielding. We consigned it to the rear of the fireplace and in the course of a week burned it to ash, then recovered the wedges.

Kitchen heat was by means of a gas cookstove and its oven when desired. The door to the bathroom could be left open to admit heat when needed, or closed when the weather turned warm. This left the bedroom.

The little utility room contained a hot water tank. Its heater was a bit of an oddity, being a small coal-burning stove about four feet high and two feet in diameter, its top section a jacket where water about it was heated and returned to the tank. Its fuel was coal, anthracite, that burned with no smoke and a blue flame. Once ignited, it would continue afire for a few days. We added more coal about once a day, as needed. The little stove had to be kept burning constantly if one desired hot water, and one did. In fact, two did.

We had come from bituminous coal country and found anthracite to be a challenge. If we left for a few days to visit family or any other reason, our return found the fire had ceased, necessitating its rekindling. Now, anthracite is a hard material resembling small chunks of steel-black granite. Igniting it was about as difficult as though it *were* granite. I found this so time and again. The process frustrated my sweetheart to tears on more than one occasion.

When bedroom heat was needed, the door to the utility room was left open, and its small exterior window, closed. In warm weather the position of the two was reversed, although heat still entered the bedroom, whose windows could be opened to admit fresh, outside, cooling air. This was our thermostat, an *armstrong* model: it required application of strong arms.

Spring arrived. My call to military duty came. Initially it required attendance at a Basic Officers' school at Fort Monmouth, a comfortable driving distance down the road. And graduation came by, toward the end of May. My mother came as a guest, both of the graduation and of our abode. We offered her the use of the bedroom, and camped on the sofa in the living room during her few days' visit.

The weather had turned nicely warm. Of course, hot water was desired, so we kept the little stove well stoked, lest it burn out and require the tedious rekindling process. We prepared the bedroom for the night, with the little utility room window open, its door closed, and bedroom windows open. After the evening's chatter, mother retired for the night. Joyce and I did the same.

Morning came. Everyone took turns in the single bathroom, mother first, then Joyce, then I. We sat for breakfast at the small living room table next to the kitchen. More family conversation continued. In the process mother said how *hot* it was in the bedroom last night. We wondered why: we had noticed no such discomfort.

And then she told us she had opened a closet door, found it not a closet, and closed the bedroom windows for fear of someone breaking in. I looked. She had opened the utility room door, left it quite ajar, and with the bedroom windows closed, about roasted to death.

At least let it be said: we gave her a warm welcome. Indeed.

Michael Toia

FLY BALL

F ootball, baseball, basketball, and to perhaps a lesser extent remaining sports, are part and parcel of the fiber, the psyche, of many. Our TV service has hundreds of cable channels carrying everything from the Superbowl, the World Series, down to local high school lacrosse games. And indeed these channels exist because there is a good-sized audience for this fare and commercials intermixed in the broadcast produce a profit for the advertiser.

However, my brain is somewhat miswired: I harbor but a mild interest in team sports. To me, sport is taking a canoe that you don't want anymore, to a raging river known for its appetite for such things, put in, paddle along, and see how long you can survive, one on one against beastly currents.

So it was as I, a young boy, grew to my mid teens. Science and "geekdom" drew me through early life, education, and interest. Always last pick in school athletic classes when sports teams were formed, I remained a poor performer. High school days would find a gym class running a basketball up and down the court, and I could hardly ever score, defend well, or contribute to the game, other than to get plenty of exercise.

On warm days coach would take us outdoors to a softball field. My team invariably placed me way out, in right field, a spot of little activity.

Now, our class had a few super jocks, the type who excelled at every sport, and a fine fella, a 6' 4" or so African-American, Kenny, was one such. I was never chosen to be on the super jock team. And when Kenny came to bat, he would usually put the ball waaay up, up and away, practically out of sight, and right out deep into right field, mine to handle.

I could not field that ball, but waited for its return, its hitting the dirt, retrieved it and hurled it as far as I could. It bounced along to the second baseman. By that time Kenny had already rounded the bases in a victory dance sort of way. He joked about me, and I took it good naturedly: we were reasonable friends.

That's how I spent my sophomore year.

I had a very good friend, Jack. We were all but inseparable. Both obtained ham radio licenses about that time, two geek types. But jack did enjoy softball, and we spent a lot of time tossing the ball back and forth when on our own time outdoors.

One noteworthy incident about Jack remains in memory. We were at a gathering of radio hams, a thousand or so, at a county park. A softball game was organized, and at Jack's wish, we joined in. I played my usual right field, and Jack, center field.

During one at-bat, the opposing team's slugger drove that ball fast, furious, and out to center field. Jack ran in, deeply intent on fielding the thing, but overdid it: the ball was about to fly overhead and behind him. He realized this, abruptly dug in his heels, tried to spin about, but could not compensate in time. He removed his glove, and with a disgusted and loud grunt of "Ratz!" threw it into the air, toward the ball.

Of all things, the ball hit the glove, right in the pocket, and the thereby-merged duo began a descent back to earth, Jack running beneath. In a stunning feat, he caught both! An Out! Everyone was amazed, none more than Jack himself.

That summer found us tossing the ball as usual, and Jack would often pitch to himself, tap it with a bat, for a short fly ball, very easy to catch, and I would do so. He and a few others taught me how to follow through with a bare-handed catch, so as to arrest the ball with a sort of net made of the fingers of both hands. We practiced this every day, rather often. And as the summer wore on, I found I could field his flys with a single hand, and enjoyed doing so.

Well, Jack got to putting a little more steam into his slugging a bit at a time, the ball taking a higher and farther flight, and I would field it. We got good at this little game, and had a lot of companionship and exercise thereby.

The summer wore on. September began along with school. Days slouched toward Indian Summer: warm, dry, sunny. Gym class found us out on the softball field. Again I was last pick on the un-super jock team. I was assigned right field. History simply repeated itself, following its standard template.

The teams took their places, and their turns at bat. Not far into the game Kenny came to bat. Our pitcher could never get the ball past him. And surely, Kenny connected with as mighty a "whap" as ever. The ball shot into the sky, up, up, and of course deep over right field. I saw it, followed it, and it began its bomb-like descent.

It was airborne quite a while, thus allowing ample time to position myself. And as it continued the last phase of its flight, it dropped right toward me. Thanks to Jack's summer of training, I made a single-hand "snatch catch." In fact, it felt easy, natural. I then held the ball overhead, in a somewhat triumphal display. Kenny had rounded third and was headed home. Coach said, "OUT!" Kenny said, "WHAT! What you mean, 'OUT?' " Coach said, "He caught the ball!"

Kenny was just about to cross home plate. He turned, saw me in my victory pose. He picked up a bat, and began a serious run across the field, right toward me, swinging that bat, and uttering a goodly quantity of very angry words. Oh boy – trouble. RUN!

Dropping the ball, I spun about, and with a freshly prepared, enormous shot of adrenalin, began a sashay outbound. In a very short order an 8-foot chain link fence approached me. How, I do not know, but I was over it in two seconds, yet cranking up more steam in my gait. It slowed Kenny down a bit more, but failed to stop him.

We continued along the fence, toward the school building, around it, and back toward home plate. Kenny was right on my tail. I ran by the coach. As Kenny followed, coach tripped him. Kenny hit the dirt. Coach was right on top of him, and screamed, "A HUNDRED PUSHUPS!"

Kenny was now panting. I had slowed, stopped, and fell to the ground, at last out of danger, breath, and adrenalin. Kenny and coach had a short discussion:

Kenny: "But coach…"

Coach: "TWO hundred!"

Kenny: "Coach…"

Coach: "THREE hundred"

Kenny: "Coach…"

Coach: "FOUR hundred. And an extra five hundred for poor sportsmanship!"

That week saw Kenny in the hall from time to time, between classes, doing his penance, coach watching. And Kenny came up to me, said, "Wow! How'd you do that?" To his great honor, we were still friends, even a tad more so.

GDI

College life has its Greek culture, Sororities and Fraternities to which one may pledge, endure an initiation process, and become accepted as a sister or brother. While this is custom, city schools garner commuting students who have neither need of housing on, nor adjacent to, campus. Many live off-campus in rental apartments, some commuting by auto, bus, or tram from their family homes. Groups of these have no time for and need of fraternal organizations, their precious daily hours devoted to a mix of classes, lab studies, homework, and commuting. Such was the case at our university: I was a commuter.

The Greek organizations carried two- or three- Greek letter abbreviations of their name. We commuters rather banded together in a clan, all having the same lifestyle, and yet some sort of social connection, one to another. We took the name of "Gamma Delta Iota" rather jokingly to our group, kept it Anglicized as GDI, an indication of our suggested name and organization: The *Goll Durned Independents*.

GDI met in the student union a few evenings a month, approved and adopted a social schedule, held routine get-togethers, assemblies, and parties.

We had no "house" per se as do the Greek societies. Ours was the student union, and gatherings were often held at places such as public and/or amusement parks, places where group activities were common. At one such we *"GollDurns"* were enjoying entertainment at a mini-golf establishment, the very evening of my heartthrob's accepting my proposal and for the first time publicly displaying an engagement ring.

The *GollDurns* was a fun loving group, the purpose of get-togethers to break away for an evening or Saturday from the grind of study, study, study. They were indeed welcome events, with about two hundred fifty souls regularly in attendance. GDI also held regular business meetings, had a formal organization recognized by the university student council, with a president, recording secretary, treasurer and so forth, meetings conducted according to Roberts Rules of Order.

Ahh, yes – order. What an interesting word. We were, after all, fundamentally out for some relief and fun, so even the monthly business meetings had need of means of conduct with decorum and order. We tried. Jocular outbursts were common, and GDI's president would repeatedly rap his gavel on the table, call the meeting back to order so we could proceed.

In my senior year the president-elect was a man good with managerial skills, a military demeanor, and as it happened, likely majoring in ROTC, the Reserve Officers' Training Corps – kiddingly, of course. The university, tho hosting Army ROTC, did not offer a major in that field.

At the end of the academic year, a GDI meeting was assembled to elect a slate of officers for the coming year. Most of GDI's members were present in a large ballroom at the union, intent on conduct of business and at the same time socializing, enjoying the end of the semester and company of mutual friends and clan members.

7:30 PM: the president called us to order. Candidates for the various offices had earlier been nominated and had been running for office. Proceedings got underway. Candidates' names were tabulated and presented to the clan. Then we moved on to the voting process.

The scene was that of a parliamentary procedure akin to what one witnesses from time to time in Great Britain: much boisterous commentary, a reasonable amount of disorder accompanying the process, tho in the clan it was of a friendly, non-contentious nature. Various groups extolled the virtues of their chosen nominees. Ayes of approval, some guffawing and general enthusiasm kept the meeting quite lively.

The president needed to restore order time and again. We would hear his gavel, and his voice, in a military manner, command "At Ease!" This, of course, is the military term to knock off all the commotion and return to a relaxed, but quiet and attentive state.

Over and over again we would hear the admonition, "At Ease" and after each, as the crowd quieted down, our good friend Ed, a grad student in Chemical Engineering, countered in a loud, polite, clarion voice, heard by all, at a slow, deliberate cadence: "Mister President, Sir: the word is 'ORDER!' " This exchange between the two happened so frequently I lost count of its occurrences. It did so about every two to three minutes for the majority of the meeting, well into two hours. After every expression of exuberance by the group, one heard, "At Ease! At Ease!" followed by "Mister President, Sir: the word is 'ORDER!' "

Ed was persistent. Not being an ROTC student, he seemingly requested, perhaps demanded, we follow the accepted procedures in Roberts Rules of Order. And at long last, his exhortations, his continual incantation, got through to the president. On yet another outburst, toward the end of the evening, the president changed his vocabulary, shouting "Order! Order!"

As the crowd came back to reasonable control and quiet once again settled thereupon, the clarion voice, that that had been offering the correctional admonition time and again, rang out: "Two Beers!"

This disrupted the proceedings for nigh onto ten minutes. Ed's tenacity had prevailed. He had laid a trap, baited it continually, fresh bait offered every few minutes, and the president eventually took it, upon which the trap was sprung. It was a good lesson in how to work your fish and land him, too. A memorable meeting it was, indeed, one evening circa 1960, and this writing being in the year of our Lord 2018. To this day I yet hear Ed's voice in my mind's ear, as I recall his warm friendship.

　　　　　　　　Michael Toia

SELFOSS

1.   Independence

T ommy was a colleague and close friend, and Danish born. He emigrated to Utah at age 14 speaking little or no English. This I was told. It was not at all evident in his speech, mannerisms, expressions, or bearing. In everyway he was an American, with quite better than average vocabulary, elocution, and command of the U. S. version of English. It was only after months of working together and the building of a warm friendship that I came to know his heritage. We two were senior engineers at our workplace, both approaching retirement age.

A story he related concerned Hitler's takeover of Europe in the forties. The Nazi Forces invaded country after country, in the mode as so succinctly put by Rush Limbaugh: by breaking things and killing people.   Poland, Czechoslovakia, France, Italy, fell under Nazi rule. German U-boats prowled the Atlantic, taking a heavy toll on shipping from North America to the Allied forces in Britain. Hitler lusted to control Iceland, to have it as a convenient submarine base half way across the ocean, an efficient place from which to conduct U-boat operations.

As World War II broke out, Iceland was under Danish government, a protectorate or colony or some such: the actual designation escapes me. Hitler set his sights on Denmark, sent his armies and air forces to subjugate the country. Tommy continued his story. King Christian X, ruler of the country at that time, *welcomed* the Nazis as a group of friends, tourists, bade them stay as long as was their desire, and enjoy the country. Apparently not a shot was fired, nothing was bombed or destroyed. The king, in this manner, spared his people much unnecessary bloodshed and misery. The people saw his plan and adopted it willingly. The Nazi's took control of the government and the King remained in power, subservient to them. That was April 9, 1940.

So now Hitler had his prize! Iceland! And so easily, as well. But, as Frost so eloquently penned, *"The best laid plans O' mice and men gang aft agley."* And agley they did gang. [5] Britain, realizing the gravity of the situation, invaded and occupied Iceland a month and one day later, on May 10. It, too, was a bloodless takeover. Occupation passed to the United States a year and one month later.

Iceland protested, but in a defensive mode, tolerated the Allied forces, who provided protection as they established air and naval bases there to counter the Nazi operations in the North Atlantic. In this way the island nation became about 90 percent literate in English.

Then, on June 17, 1944, Iceland declared its independence from Denmark. The king's response was along the lines of, "Bless you, my former people and friends. Enjoy your new country. Prosper. Keep in touch."

For years I had entertained the thought of visiting the country, a sort of wish-list wanderlust, "wandering" what it might be like. Earlier I had purchased a book, *Teach yourself Icelandic*, and was looking though the constructs of the language. Tommy encouraged me. "Go! Go to Reykjavik. You'll love it." This further fueled my lust of wander. My desire to do so welled up.

---

[5] Gang, I postulate, is related to the German verb *gehen*, to go, conjugated as *gehen, ging, ist gegangen, geht.*

2.   Madness

As if the fates conspired quite shortly thereafter, Air Iceland offered a travel package, a *Midwinter Madness* trip to Iceland, four days, three nights at one of their tourist hotels in Reykjavik. The price for two was so reasonable, so tempting. Spouse Joyce and I discussed it one evening, and the next morning she had scheduled the trip. We were to leave February 9. Winter in Iceland? Madness indeed.

Excitedly I phoned: "Tommy! Guess what! We're going to Reykjavik next week! Quick! Give me some pointers on the language!" I gushed away. He answered, "You'll love it. But why do you think I can help you with the language?"

"Well," I replied, "Iceland was Danish until World War II. Isn't the language the same?"

His answer? *"Four Hundred **Years** ago."*

Rats! That wasn't much help. But at the anointed hour we were off. I carried my *teach yourself* book along, hoping it might come in handy. A six hour flight from Baltimore saw us to Keflavik airport, where a waiting bus inhaled us, fellow passengers, and an hour later deposited all at our hotel.

It was cold. Not overly so, but a brisk wind recommended one keep one's overcoat well buttoned up. We checked in, got to our room, then joined others in the dining room for the evening's meal. Finally! We were in Reykjavik. Another punch list item accomplished.

Our six hour flight, the time zone shift of five hours and the bus trip consumed all of that short winter day. We departed the dining room at its closing time, strolled through the lobby, then returned to our room on the third of the hotel's six floors. As the hours passed, the wind picked up. Considerably. Lying in bed we could feel the room sway back and forth a bit. Our one large window so bulged in and out with the gusts so as to be cause for alarm. Will it shatter?

My protective instinct drove me from bed. It was as on a cruise ship, the deck swaying just a bit, enough to instill an uneasy feeling.

Uneasy? More at fearful! Stepping into my trousers, socks and shoes, and donning a shirt, I left the room, did somewhat of a "drunk walk" down the swaying corridor to the elevator, descended to the lobby and approached the front desk. A woman was on duty. Inquiring about the building's safety elicited a calming response. It's that way every evening.

I stepped outside to witness the wind, and found it necessary to lean at rather a good angle to avoid being blown over backward. Perhaps this is how Iceland was first populated: a few Norse fishermen ventured too far off shore, were picked up buy that breeze and deposited a few hours after on this country's shore. It may have taken them a year to do the upwind return trip. Just a guess.

3.   Reykjavik

T he next day we rented a small car. Quite small. Smaller than the VW "bug" or the Smart Car, more on the order of the three-cylinder-engine *Geo Metro* that appeared in the States for a short time. But it was dependable transportation. Equipped with a map of the area we set out, Joyce navigating and I at its controls.

It was confusing, the street signs being in Icelandic, with names such as Kringlumyrarbraut, Skeiðargogur, Langholtsvegur and the like. We could not fathom how to properly pronounce most of them, and were attempting to keep up with traffic. By the time I tried to pronounce one, and Joyce found it on the map, we had passed by three others. We pulled over at a parking spot and devised a plan: I would just say the first and last letter of each and she would try to navigate. That strategy proved quite successful.

We found our way to the local mall, and later to the downtown shopping area. Joyce strolled from store to store, I following, gathering the various packages as they began to accumulate. She delighted in the shopping experience but did not buy much, just an item here and their for friends back home, plus a souvenir or two. The evening was as usual breezy, and a light drizzle fell. Streets were devoid of ice and snow. It doesn't get that awfully cold there, despite the latitude of 65 plus degrees North. I presume the passing Gulf Stream tempers the climate.

Next came time to seek sustenance. We drove along the shopping area streets, spied an interesting looking bistro, and fate provided a single parking spot immediately in front. With the auto thus granted a bit of rest, we exited, crossed the sidewalk and ascended the six or so steps to the establishment's front door. A tall, young maître'd met us, said in perfect North American neutral English, "Good evening, folks. Bar or meal?" We opted for the latter. He escorted us to a cozy table in a warm spot. we asked, "Do you have a menu?" His answer: "Yes - it's in Icelandic," to which we replied, "OK – what's good?" He made a few recommendations, and our order was in.

We sat, chatted a bit, relating our impressions of the country to each other. The ambiance was comfortable, warm. Our overcoats dried off a bit. The experience was definitely European. Iceland considers itself an extension of, and a part of, Europe. Joyce commented, "This is just as good as being in Paris." I agreed. Then she added, "It's better. There aren't any haughty French criticizing our dress and speech."

Dinner wrapped up, the evening came to an end. It had been an interesting day and a once-in-a-lifetime learning experience. By and by we made it back to the hotel and set in for a night's rest and sleep. The wind picked up. The floor again rendered to us that feeling of being at sea. But we had begun accepting it, worried not, and did get a good night's rest.

4.   Communication

M orning came. Somewhat late. Owing to the nation's keeping Greenwich Mean Time as civil time, and its longitude of about 20 degrees West, aggravated by the shorter winter day and high Northerly latitude, dawn broke near ten AM. We had a bit of breakfast at the hotel dining room. Fare was a mix of a bit of American, catering to the tourist trade, and a bit more Icelandic. Cod was one offering. It was declined.

The day's plan was to visit a few landmarks. Gullfoss, the large waterfall, was to the East, and we judged about a two hours' drive. Not far removed squirts Geysir, the world's second largest at one of the island's many geothermal fields. We set our site on a visit to both. We exited the hotel and inserted ourselves into the mini-car to start on our way, gassing up before leaving Reykjavik's area. We believed, correctly as it happened, that gasoline stations could be few and far between.

A bit after daybreak found us rolling out Iceland Route One, headed East, about an hour's drive, and then to the North along Route 36. On the way we passed a roadside sign, *Hester*. I recognized it as one of the two words in my knowledge of the language: *Horse*. There was a sort of dude ranch off to the South and a tad down the way.

Route 36 was a two-lane, mostly paved road, but gave way to reasonably travelable black, volcanic dirt in spots. We drove, I at the wheel, Joyce navigating from our not-too-detailed map. Eventually we reached a crossroad, decided Geysir was to the right, and turned accordingly, apprehensively. In that very small crossroads village there appeared a large parking lot at what was likely a bed and breakfast, or a guesthouse of sorts. Joyce suggested we stop and ask directions. I set aside my macho male instincts, and willingly submitted to her wisdom.

Now, there we were, out in the country, in the dead of winter, a bit of light snow about, East of a low mountain range to the West of which lay Reykjavik. Neither of us has any facility at all with Icelandic. Further, the establishment was closed, not another auto in the lot. I pulled up fairly close to its obvious main entrance. Joyce stepped out, walked up to the door and knocked. Shortly a woman appeared. Joyce tried to communicate our unfamiliarity with the area and our desire to visit Geysir. The exchange did not last long. She returned, entered the auto, and said, "Go back to the road we just left, turn right, go about one km, turn right, go about 5 km, and turn left. You can't miss it."

I was amazed! Wow! "You understand Icelandic? You were able to express our situation and understand her instructions? How?" Joyce said, "She spoke English."

5   Geysir

The auto was turned about, driven back to the road we had been on, and turned right to continue as had been directed. In the half-mile stretch we did find the next road, turned right, followed the given directions to a left turn, and indeed, ran right into the small village at Geysir. It contained a gasoline station, a tourist lodge with gift shop and a few other buildings. Joyce did her thing in the gift shop. I filled the tank, parked, and walked right ahead into the geothermal field, camera in tow.

Geysir, second in height of its spurt only to the one at Steamboat Springs, Colorado, was close at hand. It was steaming a bit. I waited. The signage, in a few languages including English, told that its eruptions are random, not timely as is Old Faithful. I hoped. I waited.

Nearby bubbled a collection of a dozen or so small geysers. They performed rather regularly, squirting hot water some ten or so feet into the air every few minutes. With camera deployed and waiting, I set about capturing the scene. The path leading to this small assortment actually ran through its middle, a half dozen or so on either side. One behind me would squirt for five seconds. I spun about, but it ceased before the camera shot could be taken. Meanwhile others formerly to my front did the same. I spun about again, with the same result.

Those two groups of little devils so teased me for ten to twenty minutes. But time drew nigh. Sunset approached and could not be denied. Joyce hailed me from the walkway's entrance. We returned to the car, she with a sweater of a particular pattern that had been her quest, and we were off, to seek out Gullfoss.

That geologic feature was nearby, a double cascade of a small river into a bit of a canyon. We parked, walked to its overlook, took photos. As waterfalls go, it was quite impressive. Not the largest we had seen, but different, with ample water roaring into the chasm, and well worth the trip. Crowds were manageable: we were its sole visitors! It reminded me of a visit to a small waterfall decades earlier, on our Poconos honeymoon. We were wed New Year's Eve. The Poconos are closed in winter, just as was this feature.

6.   Country Dining

T he sun angle forebode the coming of dark. We again returned to our minicar and drove off. And surely, night enshrouded us as we found our way back to Route 36. It was yet about an hour's drive to Highway One, and nothing was open along the route: there existed nothing that *could* be.

As a diabetic I am advised to eat small portions several times daily. Could we make it back to Reykjavik before a sugar low took its toll on my body and eyesight? Joyce studied the map. A town of possibly reasonable size was not too far to the East. Surely there should be someplace offering food, even if just a small grocery store. Our course was set for that village: Selfoss.

Reaching its western edge a half-hour East of Route 36, we beheld a beautiful sight, a small bridge across the river, suspended from cables between its two main towers, all festooned in white lights. The roadway signs in Icelandic thankfully included highway and street numbers to enable following our route. An as we approached the bridge, myself at the controls, Joyce said, "There's a restaurant!" It was a surprise: I had no idea of how to say, or spell, *restaurant* in the native language.

Nor was there need. To the right, just a few blocks to the south stood a Cape Cod type structure with its goodly pitched gable roof. Along the entire length of its ridge stood a sign about two feet tall. It heralded: R E S T A U R A N T. Even I could interpret it.

In just a few moments the route to the building was easily navigated. Our auto again entered a well-earned rest period. We exited, walked to the building, were greeted, shown to a table, relaxed, and dined quite well. Ambiance was nicely comfortable. There was respite from the cold. Soft music played in the background. The meal was unhurried, pleasing and satisfying. That restaurant, well East of Reykjavik, was warm, welcome, wonderful – and THAI! But we were well into Iceland! How did *that* happen?

7.   Blue Lagoon

A fter dinner it was off again, to our return trip: Reykjavik and the hotel. We arrived about 9 PM and had by that time set about a plan for the next day: visit the famous Blue Lagoon, a geothermal spring and spa area.

Morning breakfast and inquiry at the front desk gave us the sustenance and information required to initiate that plan. It was about an hour's drive somewhat West through geothermal fields that led to the site. We approached. All about was harsh, jagged, black volcanic ash, much of it with a jet black, glassy, vitreous appearance. A paved walkway though its field led from a parking lot to the facility. We beheld a rather large, new, and beautiful structure, the equal of many a high end hotel or restaurant. But this was a spa.

The facility had standard tourist accommodations: a small restaurant, gift shop, and I believe rooms for overnighters. Beyond a huge glass wall was seen the blue lagoon itself, a large geothermal "hot tub." Although it was the dead of winter, a few dozen people were out in the waters, a light steam mist rising therefrom. Water temperature is approximately 38° C, 100° F.

The water itself had the appearance of baby-blue milk, quite opaque, with an overall opalescence to it. It was so very enticing. We could scarcely contain our desire to go in for a good soaking.

It was February. We had not thought to pack our swimsuits!

The return to Reykjavik was pleasant. We drove slowly, taking in what sights were there for enjoyment. A geothermal electrical power plant sat in the vicinity. It happens that a fair percentage of the nation's power is so derived. But we saw no evidence of large coal, gas, or oil fired plants. My engineering curiosity drove me later to look up stats on Iceland, particularly their electricity. It seems some eighty percent is obtained from hydro plants ... water power.

The remainder of the evening saw us once again to a large shopping mall, in browse mode as most if not all of our souvenir purchases had by that time been completed. A nice supper and return to the hotel led to our repacking for our trip back home, scheduled for the next day. The evening wind again rocked us to sleep.

8.   Su n s e t

M orning, the day of our final visit to the island nation, rousted us from our slumber. After a bit of breakfast, we set off to do just a bit more sightseeing, and finally turned in the rental car. A short taxi ride brought us back to the hotel. We met others about to head to the States, chatted a bit with fellow travelers, then boarded the bus for transportation to Keflavik, and followed the standard drill to board an airplane. Everything went smoothly. Bags were checked. The security check found nothing out of order. We climbed aboard, found our seats and settled back. Shortly the engines wound up, the craft's taxi maneuvers began, and in a wee bit we lifted off, into a beautiful sunset scene. It was 5:20 PM local time.

Joyce and I chatted a bit about our experiences, how we thoroughly enjoyed this *midwinter madness* excursion, the sights, the foods, the language. Out the window, sunset was yet in progress. We had been airborne a half hour. And as we continued our flight Westbound toward Baltimore, the sunset remained, as if simply painted on the sky itself. This continued for two and a half hours! What was happening? Had my wristwatch gone haywire? Was it racing ahead in time? But logic prevailed ...

The earth's equator is about 24,000 miles around. Anyone standing thereon races eastward at 24,000 miles in 24 hours, or a thousand miles per hour. Our takeoff latitude was over 60 degrees North. A circle of that constant latitude has a length half that of the earth's circumference, or 12,000 miles. Thus Keflavik airport races eastward at a bit under 12,000 miles in 24 hours, or slightly less than 500 miles per hour as the earth rotates.

Great circle navigation put us on a Westerly course for a few hours. Although the sun was moving 500 miles per hour to the West of someone on the ocean directly beneath us, we were traveling westward at 500 miles per hour. We were chasing the sun, and keeping up with it for the first few hours.

Eventually the course turned more Southward, and our net speed to the West diminished, presenting for our enjoyment a beautiful sunset in very slow motion, taking about three and a half hours to completion. It was yet another spectacle to recall from our trip.

Visit Iceland? Mid winter? Yes! Tommy was so right. If the opportunity arises, go! You'll love it. I have yet to visit some summertime, but it's on my list.

THE WALL

A lexandria, an old, colonial-time city on the banks of the Potomac, was a thriving business center when George Washington was yet young. Today it rests a scant few miles downstream from the nation's capital, Washington D.C. We lived nearby, and workdays commuted to our jobs in that capital. It was our custom to drive the few miles to Alexandria, park the car, walk but a few blocks to a bus line and continue, reversing the procedure in the evening.

The drive was pleasant, interesting. The small city abounds with history. Geologically it sits among low, rolling hills, giving the roadways a certain charm. George Washington slept here. Really. And on multiple occasions. He also ate, drank, shopped there, along streets now lined with quite mature trees, I dare say some having witnessed the man himself.

Near the riverfront a few streets are paved with rounded cobbles, reputedly the ballast stone carried by empty ships arriving to load cotton, tobacco and other products of Virginia Colony. Several others are paved with stone or brick. The sidewalks over which we strode were paved with very old brick or flagstone.

.Many led past fieldstone walls, a few feet high, holding back the soil and lawn of aged estates. Even the walks were usually pleasant, wonderful in spring and fall, not too cold in winter, but a bit trying in summer.

In that season the Washington area is known historically for its temperature and humidity, both with numbers in the 90's. It can be unpleasant, and difficult to breath at times. One would develop a good sweat with the lightest of exercise. Tho it is uncomfortable, it's not nearly as being in Houston in summer, where temperatures climb to 100 and the Gulf of Mexico, that grand old lady, picks up her petticoat of humidity, tiptoes over the city, then lowers it as a blanket of oppressively unbreatheable air for days at a time.

The sidewalks had another old-town characteristic. Over the decades as the trees matured, their root systems followed suite, and lifted the stone or brick pavers irregularly here and there. One's passage often took on the appearance of a drunk's walk: straight line travel was difficult to effect, it being far more convenient to follow a moderately and randomly curving route.

Those are our reminisces as a young couple, in mornings journeying into our employment as government workers, and in evenings returning home. We cherish them. We still comment on the beauty of the area, the walks, the streets, and the avenues. A particular event stands forth to this day in my mind. Our morning walk was usual, the day being the beginning of August, and humidity already at saturation although temperature was twenty or so degrees below what would be the daily high.

On our return that early evening, one of those fieldstone walls, about five feet high, had, during the day, given way, its large stones now slumped onto and occupying sufficient sidewalk that pedestrians need detour off the curb, into the bit of street and back, to pass by.

I commented: "Holy cow! Look at that!" And my lovely bride, holding my arm as she oft did in those days, added, "No wonder – with all this humidity."

ASSAULT

The Caucasian Chalk Circle is an interesting literary work by Bertolt Brecht. His more notable and famous contribution to theater is a play introducing a catchy little musical theme, "Mac the knife." But the chalk circle concerns a trial, a custody battle, between a woman of high office, a politico's wife, and a low-born common servant girl, both claiming to be a young boy's mother. It's been fifty years since its first study, and that *Auf Deutsche*. I offer this story, quite at odds with many details in the original, to illuminate only the final trial determining the boy's true mother.

Its setting is in the Caucasus of old, decades past, in the time of a nasty uprising and bloody revolution, the people turning on a corrupt government. Even the soldiers revolted, on the side of the commoners. Holders of high office – mayors, judges, governors, and on – were rounded up and executed where possible. Those missed were so because they fled and made good their escape. One such was the natural mother of a boy, an infant. She abandoned her baby, fled, leaving the little one in the care of his paid governess, a commoner, Grushe.

The revolution continued. Grushe protected the baby. She knew that, were his higher social birth known, he would be killed.

To shield him, she claimed the baby as hers, an illegitimate child, in that time a great societal disgrace and stigma. She bore the insults, that great mantle of disgrace, tending to the infant for six years.

The soldiers routed out all vestiges of corrupt government. One was a local judge. He was removed during a loud, joking, mocking rant, claiming that the town drunk could do a better job. This so caught the soldiers' fancy, that they rounded up Azdak, the town drunk, and installed him as the judge, a grand joke and insult to the former administration. [6] Azdak sat on the bench, cases being brought before him, he deciding the fates thereof, to the delight and derision of his appointers. They laughed and joked about it, so kept him there the entire time.

Things gradually settled down. The blood bath abated. Some of those who had fled began returning, one the child's natural mother, who had abandoned him years before. She sought out his governess, Grushe, found her, and demanded return of her child. But Grushe and the boy had bonded, bonded strongly, as mother and son. The boy was terrified. Grushe was torn, torn deeply, to the center of her soul. She just could not give up the boy. The true birth mother, still wealthy, was aware that the townfolk were cognizant of the story, and mindful that they would take deep umbrage at the forced reunion of child and birth mother. She took her case to court – to Azdak's court.

There were two other cases on the day's docket. A couple who had been married fifty years sought a divorce. A farmer and wife were suing a young farm hand for having raped their daughter. Azdak's court came to session. The rape case was first. Azdak did as was his custom by now, stretched his hand across the bench, palm up, and announced, "Ich nehme."

The verb, "nehmen," means *to take*. *Ich nehme* translates to *I take*, or more at *I am on the take* – I accept bribes. This had been customary for many a year, previously being "under-the-table" transactions, quiet hush-money. But discretion was a characteristic

---

[6] These details are rather at odds with the original, but are here described with a good deal of literary license.

Michael Toia

unfamiliar to Azdak. His style had initially brought roars of laughter from the soldiers, and yet did, as it mocked the earlier oppressive governing style.

The farmer approached the bench, presented an acceptable sum of money, which Azdak took, dumped on his benchtop, grunted in approval, then placed the sum beneath his robes and into his pocket. The farmer returned to his seat. Azdak addressed the farm hand. The poor youth ashamedly said he had no money, had nothing to offer. Azdak growled a grunt, told him to return to his seat. The trial began.

The farmer presented his case. In the process he introduced his daughter, appropriately dressed for the display to be presented. She took a deep, deep bow toward Azdak, revealing her very ample bosom, very ample indeed, and as had earlier been instructed, held the pose for the judge's complete acceptance and unhurried viewing. This, too, was part of the customary bribe.

On completing her performance, she stood again upright, returned to her seat. Azdak had drunk it all in. He ordered plaintiff and defendant to approach the bench. He exonerated the poor farm hand, but held the daughter over on a charge: assault with a deadly weapon!

As for the baby custody and the divorce? I need not further expound. I have made my point and told my story. The rest is history, sitting on a library shelf for your further enjoyment, and correction of the many, many details that I have forgotten but invented on the fly.

DOG TALE

This is a classic story in the world of electricity and electrical gadgets. Is it true? I have no idea. But it is part of the lore of telephone communications.

* * * * *

A pleasant, older woman, widowed several years, lived alone in the home her husband had left her. She was well established in her church and the town, with an active social life and a group of close friends. The telephone was an important instrument in her life, whereby social events, news, happenings, medical appointments and goings-on were brought to her attention, to be annotated on a large wall calendar hanging nearby. The calendar, in fact, was part and parcel of her social diary. The phone's ring was a frequent, welcome event throughout the day.

With the woman lived a dog of fair size who was not a hunter, but rather a close friend, her pet, more at a member of the family. She and dog were all but inseparable. Wherever she went, dog went. He was trained, quite intelligent, and of the type dog lovers recognize as being able to understand human language. Scoff not. It is true. We ourselves had just such a pet many years ago, named Duchess, or Dutch for short. Through her I give an example of a dog's intelligence:

I was in the Army. Wife and I lived in an off-Post neighborhood housing many other Army personnel. I was on-Post each day. Wife tended management of the household. She and several other Army wives befriended each other, and mutual visits to their homes were common.

One warm day duties concluded mid afternoon, and I arrived home a few hours ahead of schedule. I entered the driveway. Dutch was resting beneath a bush next to the few front steps, heard me, came out, and greeted me with a wagging tail and a light bark. We nudged one another, I gave her a good petting, then ascended the steps to the porch. Dutch followed and in short order we were in the living room.

I called my wife's name once: twice: no reply. She was not home, probably nearby visiting a friend. I removed my boots, socks and shirt, fetched a glass of water, changed the water in Dutch's bowl, and returned to the living room to relax on the sofa. Dutch stayed at my side throughout.

On the coffee table sat a small note pad of the sort used to send social greetings to another, along with matching envelopes. A pen rested alongside. With a comical idea springing to mind, I made out a note: "Joyce – I'm home. We finished early today. No rush. Come at your convenience. Love ya." Dutch watched intently.

I put the note in an envelope, closed the flap, and wrote "JOYCE" on the outside. Walking to the screen door with Dutch following, I addressed the dog, opened her jowls, placed the note inside, closed her mouth, opened the screen, and commanded, "GO SEE JOYCE!"

Dutch was off as though shot from a cannon! She bounded down the steps, across the yard, and I watched as she ran a block and a half, then turned a corner and was out of sight. I laughed out loud to myself, thought that the note would be dropped when she passed the next fire hydrant, returned to the sofa and relaxed with the morning paper.

In several minutes Dutch was back, on the porch, barked, barked again, and a third time. I commanded, "Quiet, Dutch! I'm trying to relax." But she continued, and would not cease despite a repeated command to do so. I rose, went to the door, and saw Dutch pushing something along the floor with her nose. It was the envelope!

I let Dutch into the house, retrieved the note, and examined it. As one would guess, it contained a fair helping of dog slobber. But on the envelope itself was written, "I'm visiting Babs – be home in a wee bit," in Joyce's handwriting! Amazing! Dutch actually did what I jokingly commanded, and even brought back a reply!

Many readers will be skeptical and not believe this, but it is as true as the Sunrise in the morning. Our dear sweet pet did understand me, and took what I intended as a joke totally to heart as a command, and carried it out.

A bit later Joyce came up the steps, crossed the porch and entered the room, to my waiting arms and a kiss. She exclaimed exuberantly, "You'll never guess what happened! I was visiting Babs, in her kitchen, having a cup of coffee. Dutch came to the rear door and started growling! She wouldn't stop until I got up and went out the door to see what was wrong. She had a note in her mouth, from *you*. Babs and I were stunned. I wrote on the envelope that I'd be home soon, and put it in Dutch's mouth."

I handed Joyce the wet envelope. "This little thing?" Joyce about fell over, saying, "My gosh! She brought it back!" Yes, Dutch really did. And amazed the two of us. From about that day forward we would sometimes resort to spelling out a word, for fear Dutch could understand everything we said! Some canines are indeed intelligent pets.

So it was with the widow's pet. He was a wonderful companion, would fetch various things on voice command, and was a true friend, not to mention protector as well. He was, well ... family.

Dogs need to run outside at times. Their owners often walk them, and the widow did so frequently. She also had a dog run in her yard, a steel wire, one end attached to the house, and the other to a tree. A pulley on the wire held a light chain, the far end of which attached to a metal choker-type chain collar that fits loosely about a dog unless he is pulling hard. The house attachment was to a metal hose bib meant for attachment of a garden hose. Beneath was a water bowl for dog.

A time came that the phone seemed not to ring much, if at all. And when the widow spoke to friends, they said they had been trying to call but got no answer. Yet she had no trouble placing calls. The phone obviously was in order. Friends began to suspect the widow might be shunning them, but she strongly and genuinely protested this.

At the same time, when dog was outside confined to the run, he would occasionally yelp and let out a most unusual, tormented cry. It was unexpected, and the widow was concerned. When she heard his cry, she went to his aid. But before she could reach him, and after several such yelps, he stopped, lay on the ground, writhing a bit, and panting.

This continued for a spell. After the third or so time, she went to the phone to call the vet for an appointment. But as she picked up its handpiece, there was a friend on the line, calling, though the instrument had not rung. Most curious.

Widow became accustomed to this unusual behavior. Dog had become prescient, having developed this manner of announcing that someone was calling, although the phone rang not. In fact, it did not ring at all, even with dog inside, but dog lost his sensing ability while indoors.

Widow contacted "*Ma Bell*," the telephone company. In those days telephone service was provided by a regulated monopoly, the Bell Telephone company. She reported that her phone no longer rang, but it was not a critical issue, as dog had the ability to announce when someone was calling.

Shortly thereafter came a repairman to put the phone in proper order. He verified that its ringer did not function. Now I explain a bit about technology of the day. A pair of copper wires connected the telephone to cabling outside the house, and on, through to the telephone switchboard, and to the phone on the other end. Voices were carried as weak electrical vibrations on the pair. The ringer, on the other hand, worked by connecting the pair together, and placing about 100 volts of alternating current on them, measured against earth ground. A single *ground* wire connected the phone instrument to a good earth ground, usually the building water pipe that enters from the street. This effected the ringer.

The repairman measured the ground connection. It was faulty. He traced it to the basement where it was, in fact, securely attached to a metal water pipe. He continued, tracing the water pipe back toward the street. And he found that a repair had been made next to the pipe's street end. The metal pipe had apparently failed, and a plumber had replaced a section of it with plastic pipe. This interrupted the ground connection. He re-established it by placing a jumper wire from the street end to the other end of the metal water pipe. With that the phone ringer functioned once again.

But dog had lost his prescience. He no longer announced incoming phone calls. And it's a good thing, too. With the ground connection interrupted by the plastic pipe, the ringer voltage appeared on the house water pipe, the hose bib, the dog run wire, the pulley and chain, and choker collar. With each incoming call, poor dog was being zapped by the ringer voltage! And any older telephone man can attest, that the ringer signal, 100 volts at 20 cycles, yields a very unpleasant, painful shock!

EXIGENCY

Weather was pleasant, not overly hot, less humid than usual. A stroll about the wood, the thin, young pine forest and its companion open areas of sparsely grassy field seemed inviting. But it was more. It was one of our continual inspection tours as the Lieutenant and I, a Captain, participated in a fielded Army Reserve unit during their two-week active duty call to summer camp. We were "ground-pounders," the lapels of our uniforms displaying the crossed flags of the Signal Corps. The unit had deployed its several small, mobile communications vehicles about the area and were conducting drills, exchanging military *traffic*, as messages are called, with others of their kind elsewhere.

On one small truck rested a shelter housing a telephone switchboard, five troops assigned to keeping it running 'round the clock, its function belied by a few bundles of field wire leading off into the distance. Its single on-duty operator continued his function, and the others exchanged salutes as we approached. I let the Lieutenant conduct a short inspection, as it was necessary that he, too, receive his share of training.

Besides our usual uniform of rifle, canteen, ammo belt, and appurtenances thereupon, we carried a small additional pack: a few hand tools of the trade and a military field telephone. We departed the vehicle and crew, continued along toward another, following one of the wire bundles. In highly fluid tactical situations these communications cables are hastily laid directly on the ground, in parallel rows before fanning out to their differing destinations. Standard care is taken to hang them overhead at road crossings, lay them in ditches alongside a road, and/or pass them through culverts beneath.

At one point we came across a telephone pair, as the two wires twisted together are called, this one rising from the ground up a tree to effect a road crossing. To continue our personal training, we drew from our field pack a standard Signal Corps knife, scraped a bit of insulation from the two wires, then attached them to companion terminals on the field phone. We were able to listen in to the circuit, use our phone to send supervisory signals such as "off hook," indicating to a switchboard that we wanted to place a call.

We did so, called another inspection duo in the field, left a message for them at one of their assigned stops, then disengaged the wire, applied a bit of tape to the exposed portions and continued on our way. We had satisfied ourselves that earlier training in a school-type situation does, in fact, work in the field.

The morning wore on. And bodily functions continued. It became necessary to seek out bathroom facilities. The field Army digs a fairly deep trench or hole in the earth, equips the site with rudimentary essentials. This is the latrine.

They are most often just in the open, sometimes with a six-foot or so high canvas fly wrapped about them to offer a bit of privacy. There is no roof. One did his business open to God's inspection. Quite often a wooden box of sorts was placed over each dug hole, a rudimentary toilet seat properly positioned to support the user thereof. Toiled paper sat close by, beneath an inverted large tin can as rain protection.

There was insufficient water to effect a standard flush. Solid material simply piled up in the trench, as it did in the "outhouses" of yore. Lieutenant and I completed our present mission He asked: "Do you notice the smell of smoke?" I did. Somewhere something was burning. It happened that a careless previous user, during his seating, had smoked a cigarette, then tossed the butt down the hole. And lo! It found sufficient used paper to begin smoldering.

Now this presented a bit of a problem. If the combustion remained unchecked, it might ignite the wooden superstructure and render that latrine facility unusable. Troop comfort, such as can be afforded in pseudo-combat situations, and field sanitation, are priorities of the officer corps. Lieutenant and I pondered: what course of action might address the impending problem? We had very little water on hand, with canteens about empty, and no shovel to cast dirt onto the problem area. Humans, of course, are equipped with a handy means to dispense water, the output of their kidneys and bladders. But we had already done so and exhausted our available supply. There was none left for the task at hand.

Then standard problem solving kicked in. About fifty yards off sat another small communications truck, a radio unit. We approached it at a reasonably brisk walk, and again salutes were exchanged with the operating crew, a young sergeant in charge. I asked how many men he had on hand, and how many were essential to operate the equipment for a twenty minutes period. The answers were five and one. I then issued an order: one man stay, and the remainder follow me. To the latrine we marched.

Calling attention to the smoldering incipient fire, a further order was issued: deploy what urine you can muster and direct it to the problem area. The crew gave me the weirdest of looks, but proceeded to follow the command. They were a good crew, quite up to the task, and in but a minute or so had the problem resolved. After seeing that it was so, the group was dismissed with an exchange of salutes. I offered the sergeant a "well done."

Hmmm? It's been two score years and more since that command. The crew probably yet tells their grandchildren of this crazy Captain who came marching out of the woods, commandeered them, and directed them to put out a fire in such a manner. It's a catchy story. The Lieutenant likewise probably relates the same to his grandchildren. And if they do not, I am truly surprised:

I shall.

QUIJIMINGLE

Q uite some time ago there occurred a confluence of a hardware store, a radio station, a comedy duo, and an audience. The store engaged the duo to produce a commercial, and the dialog they concocted was showered upon the audience through the medium of the airwaves.

Now, commercials hawk a product. Many are short-lived but do the job to a reasonable extent. Some make use of a clever "hook," develop a bit of a following, and as is said develop "legs." These live on in the minds of the audience, yielding return more than originally anticipated, a larger than expected "bang for the buck."

Then there are the classics, the timeless ones that never die. This is a recollection of one such commercial, aired in the summertime just shy of a half century past. I recall it clearly as if it were yesterday. The duo took on the roles of the store clerk and a customer. Customer enters, looks about, selects a product, and makes his way to the front counter. The following conversation takes place.

* * * * *

Clerk:	"Good morning, sir. Are you all right? You look sort of green."
Customer:	"Oh, I'm fine, thank you. It's my normal skin tone. I'm from Mars, actually."
Clerk:	"Good gosh! Are we being invaded?"
Customer:	"Oh, no, no. Just a shopping trip."
Clerk:	"Phew! Well then, welcome to Yoq hardware."
Customer:	"Thank you. This seems to be a friendly place and an attractive store."
Clerk:	"We do our best to keep it like that. Can I help you with anything?"
Customer:	"Ummm …Twenty feet of Quijimingle, please."
Clerk:	"Quijimingle?"
Customer:	"This green stuff here."
Clerk:	"Oh, on earth we call that garden hose."
Customer:	"Ah, good. I'll make a note of that for my next trip."
Clerk:	"Shall I wrap it?"
Customer:	"No. I'll eat it here."

* * * * *

That comic exchange has stuck with me ever since. I often shop Yoq hardware. The staff know me by name. They sometimes ask why, when I come into the place, I have this bit of a grin on my

Michael Toia

face. It's there because of that commercial, the Quijimingle, a word which to this day is, and to my grave shall be, indelibly written on my brain in bright green ink, next to the word "*YOQ.*" *That* commercial had legs. And a very appreciative customer.

INVITATION TO DANCE

A s workweeks go, there come times when out-of-town conferences need tending to. Fall of that year provided one such. So, gas up the car, pack the overnight bag, set the alarm for an earlier-than-usual time, and rise to start the required change in normal schedule. After a short but pleasant breakfast with the wife and a bit more coffee, time came. Donning the uniform of the day, a suit jacket and fall overcoat, it was out the door and into the car.

The drive was pleasant. Early morning sun set the fall colors ablaze. There was little traffic. The trip was outbound, toward a conference center about three hours' drive from city center, in the mountains to the west. Scenery went from suburban to rural. Buildings becoming smaller, yielded gradually to thinning densities of houses, then to farms where they became outnumbered by cattle and horses. The season's haying was already well underway, most of the fields already cut, with large, round bales scattered about.

Travel continued through the rolling hills, across and off the Piedmont Plateau, into the low Alleghenies. As elevation increased a bit, the moderate shift in the wood and forest became obvious. More higher-elevation tree species became prominent, with an increase in the maple population. That time of year they are unmistakable: their colors shout their very presence. But, as all good things come to an end, the mountain conference center marked the terminus of the route. It was itself in a beautiful setting in the forest with a lush understory of laurel and rhododendron.

Driving up the temporary lane, I parked, left the auto with my bags and stepped inside to the registration desk. That task accomplished with receipt of a site map and room key, a return to the car ushered it to a spot closer to my room and onto its new home for the day and the few after. I moved into my new quarters.

The conference kicked off with a business lunch, introductions one to the other, groups of eight or so seated at a table, among about a hundred attendees. The meal was good fare, and offered a chance to meet fellow conferees. We were all from the same employer, this "off-site" a means to come to know better the company organization, how different groups operated and supported one another, and to meet those outside the boundary of one's usual working environment.

Afternoon began, one presentation after another, some informative, many a massive abuse of the de-facto presentation software, in "Death by PowerPoint" sessions. Earlier in my career I myself have been led through the same assassination training. Do a presentation of what your group has accomplished in the past month. Keep it to one slide. One!

Well, trying to tell the whole story on a single slide manufactures "eye charts," so many words at quarter-point type that later are projected onto a briefing room screen at 300 pixels per inch. Each printed character is rendered at three or four pixels, little dust spots that cannot be read. The alternative is to make a very clean slide, which then portrays your work as simple, not involved, and possibly an area that can be cut to prune the budget. Damned: if you do, or if you don't – and while on the interim journey as well.

The afternoon passed. A scheduled early evening break let conferees return to their rooms and freshen up a bit. After, we assembled in the main dining area, again groups of several at a table, to continue what is known as "networking." My table mates were friends and colleagues from an earlier chapter of our employment lives. We hadn't maintained a working relationship so it was pleasant to catch up on one another's recent history.

A younger colleague and I had shared a cubbie at a previous office some years before. We exchanged information on each others' career paths. He and a group from his office had just completed a required biannual qualification program on a pistol range. We shared a mutual interest in firearms training, operation, skill, and present standings. He had been through the latest in military-style handgun weapons training, while mine had been some half-century earlier. Many changes had transpired, in weapons, ammunition, technique, and so on.

He filled me in on several of the current details. I returned the favor, my recent training being at the Frontsight Firearms Training Institute in the desert not far from Las Vegas. Wife Joyce and I are life members and recently have developed a desire to visit one week annually, in the Fall, to re-qualify with their Defensive Handgun course.

Others joined in. I was at least a quarter century their senior. They were a bit surprised that I would yet report to the range for several days and re-qualify. It seemed to command a reasonable helping of respectful admiration and a bond among us.

Replacement of the M1 Garand rifle by the M14, then the M16, the heavier weapons up to 4" mortar, and our relative skill levels became topics of conversation. My personal goal those many years ago, as a young officer and leader of men, had been to practice routinely and often, never to accept a rating less than the *expert* level for handgun, carbine, and rifle, our unit's official weapons. This, I commented, was to instill in my men not so much a bit of respect, but the desire, the *drive,* not to be outdone by a lieutenant, an ROTC 90-day wonder to boot.

It did as planned. My men aspired to, and earned, their expert ratings through a good deal of diligent work and hours on the range.

I confessed to an embarrassment committed in those early days. Having fired all morning on the M1 range and stopped for a noon feeding in the field, we returned to the firing line. The midsummer day had been hot on that Georgia post. At lunch my upper shirt had been unbuttoned a bit, to effect some cool-down. On return to the firing line, I stupidly forgot a very important rule: *button up*!

We assumed the prone position. Lane 15 was my assignment. Targets were presented. The range officer ordered: "Commence firing!" We took careful aim, peered downrange, acquired a good sight picture, squeezed out a round. Off it went. The rifle recoiled but, owing to many hours of practice, returned quickly to yield that same sight picture. A second round was squeezed off, then a third. As I continued my focus on the sights and target, the last ejected shell casing returned from overhead.

Now, ejected casings, by the rifle's design, pop out of the gun at about 30 degrees to the right of vertical. Usually. There are exceptions. And my third round was such. It popped up. Vertically. It returned the same way. Vertically. It hit the back of my helmet, which deflected it down, inside my open collar, down my back.

Shell casings leave the rifle hot. Very hot. They have just been heated by a good-sized powder charge. The experience is far from pleasant. It differs not from having a functioning soldering iron tossed down your shirt. I do not recall jumping to an erect position, just a searing, burning feeling on my back while running downrange as fast as legs would go, tugging at my shirttail, trying to outrun that shell casing and dislodge it from its position above my derriere, held there by my belt.

The range safety officer barked, "Cease Fire! Cease Fire! M1 dance on lane 15! Good show, lieutenant." The table company had a good laugh, many of them having earlier had a similar or related experience from a freshly ejected shell casing. In particular, a female neophyte has, on occasion, worn a bikini to a pistol range. Once. All too quickly she experiences a similar fate, a pistol round shell casing dropping into her cleavage, with an immediate, agitated impromptu show, sometimes a bit embarrassing. Her attire changes to much more modest dress with a buttoned-up collar in fairly short order. We learn. That branding by fire-heated brass is a well-respected and memorable teacher.

LIGHTS OUT

Newly assigned as the deputy chief of a federal laboratory, I left my previous position a third of the way across the continent and reported for duty. The change of task was to be assistant to the lab chief. There's a bit of a story as to how that came about. It's somewhat complicated and will be let to another time. Although there were others quite qualified for the position, the Chief Engineer made his selection. Tag! I was it. My wife and I packed up, tossed the dog into the car and trundled off, seven hundred miles to the East.

No one there knew me, not even the laboratory chief. It was a learning experience for all. But it went smoothly, my new boss quite tolerant of a selection forced from above, in no way a fault of mine. We established an early respect, each for the other, and he graciously accepted me, set about explaining how the facility ran, their mission, introduced the staff, and became my mentor, colleague, and friend.

The Chief Engineer, it happened, had been three levels above me for the past six years, had a few years earlier sent a small cadre to the Midwest for establishment of a new office, the cadre being about four of his employees. That had placed me in the previous job.

It was a learning experience, becoming familiar with the laboratory's filing system, its report-writing style. Duties included the mentoring of younger engineers in use of technical English, a skill others had noted in me the past decade and a half. How that came about is, and remains, yet a mystery. From first grade through college, two of my most disliked subjects were history and English. Yet there I sat: some sort of established "expert" on the subject. But the reputation did serve, and yet has served, well over the years.

The Chief Engineer had a new plan and organizational structure in mind. The laboratory was to be expanded. Considerable on-site construction greeted my arrival, a new, larger building going up. Our offices were in an old, Cape-Cod style farmhouse on the property, dating from the start of World War II. In just a few months the new building was finished, and we took occupancy thereof.

The daily routine allotted time for reading and digging through the archives. This taught the lab's history, its early beginnings, its function as part of the Radio Intelligence Division of the war, its morphing into what it now had become. The reading expedited absorbing of the customs, mannerisms, lingo, and culture of the lab, its previous work, the writing abilities of personnel still on the staff, and yielded a good appreciation of what my function was and ought to become.

One item from the archives was rather interesting and a bit unusual. A curator from the Smithsonian had visited two years earlier, and expressed an interest in acquisition of certain electronic items. Attached to his letter was a two-page, single-spaced, typewritten list of desired items, one per line. Affixed thereto was a letter of reply stating that the lab presently required and actively used all of those items. It seemed we were operating a live, functioning museum! This itself bespoke the need of modernization, part and parcel of the plan.

The new facility came on line. A grand move was put into action. Part of my duties, it happened, was to conduct an inventory of laboratory equipment. I set about the task, noting descriptions, model numbers and serial numbers of equipment as it moved about. A small yet conspicuous inventory tag was affixed to the front of each such to assist in the operation. The crew, a group of capable and cooperative engineers, technicians and assorted other help, dubbed me, and began calling me, "Tagger," a form of address rather benevolently applied and accepted.

The inventory procedure led me through a rather large storage area in the basement of one of the older buildings. There I encountered many sorts of electronic instruments, not at the moment needed, wrapped in heavy transparent plastic to keep the dust and mice at bay. One item in particular piqued my interest: a German-made radio receiver. I was, and yet remain, an ardent radio amateur, and thought perhaps it should be returned to operation and set in my office. Consultation with by boss granted a vertical nod, so another younger engineer and I set about bringing the apparatus back to life.

The files and archives held a manual for the device, written in German. Fortunately I earlier had completed several semesters of education in the language. The manual sat on my desk for a week, providing lunch hour entertainment while fueling a growing anticipation. A bit of assistance from *Cassell's* German-English dictionary, with reliance on general engineering knowledge, led to an understanding of how to power up the thing.

It was wired for standard European electrical power. One who has traveled there knows that 110 volt appliances cannot be directly plugged into their 220 volt power sockets. Some sort of converter is needed. The receiver instructions and diagrams detailed how to conveniently rearrange its innards to 110 volt power. My younger colleague and I spent a few lunch hours in the old basement accomplishing that switchover. Finally the device was ready for its long-delayed turn-on.

Next noonday we returned to the basement. My assistant, unfamiliar with technical German, asked apprehensively, "Are you *sure* you know what you're doing?" With a calm demeanor, I directed he plug the thing into a wall outlet. All was well. On the lower left side of its front panel sat a large, rotating, bar-type switch,marked EIN and AUS – German ON and OFF. It had been carefully preset to AUS when we began. I reached toward it, rotated it clockwise to EIN.

The lights went out. All lights. The basement became dark.

My friend said, "What did you do?" I didn't know myself. There was no noise, no large spark, no smell of ozone or anything burning. The lights simply went out. My first reaction? Turn the switch to AUS. Try rotating it back and forth a few times. But the lights remained off. Alright, then, we simply blew a fuse somewhere. Thankfully my younger accomplice was a smoker, so he flicked his Bic. We had light.

We made it up the stairs to the main fusebox. The building was quite old, and circuit breakers did not come into use until years after its construction. We found the fuse for the basement. It was good. But no other lights on the main floor worked. My friend inquired again, a bit more incredulously, "What *did* you do?!"

With that, we departed and walked to the new lab. It, too, was without electricity. Now, its main service came through a 480 volt, three phase, 1200 ampere panel. Surely a short circuit on that would be cause for quite some commotion. But all had been quiet. The power simply went off, everywhere on the grounds, precisely when I had manipulated that switch to EIN. My friend, yet even more incredulous, asked very emphatically, "What did you **do**?"

Now, a bit of earlier history is of interest here. At the previous office, I had developed some sort of mystical aura, had spooked a young lass computer operator so badly that she wanted to work night shift so as not to be in the building when I was about. I've related that story in a previous work, "*Frog Tongues, and other Recollections of an Old Patriarch,*" under the title SPOOKY. Her fear of me had made it through the corporate structure, and this aura had been bantered about from time to time. Apparently the staff in this laboratory had heard of it, too. My chum was rather wide-eyed but a good engineer, so did not believe in there being anything supernatural about the incident – just mysterious.

I went to my office. Routine administrivia of each working day was mine to handle. I phoned the electrical power utility to report the outage. They already knew. They said a distracted driver had just run off the road and sheared off a few utility poles at the local subsubstation. Electricity would remain off for about four hours.

A mere coincidence. The driver sheared off the poles just as I turned the switch to EIN. But my reputation as SPOOKY was enhanced a bit.

SCROOGE

Summer waned, gave way to fall. Football season got well underway. Our management had been busy the past two years planning a new regional center in the Midwest. Four of us, all middle aged male engineers, had been selected as an advanced cadre, shortly to go forth and begin building the center. We sat at headquarters, in a small office, four desks rather crowded into a room not quite sufficient for the purpose. But it was temporary.

Thanksgiving passed and the calendar heralded the approach of Christmas. Holiday spirit permeated the headquarters offices. Wreaths, small Christmas trees, holly, and assorted other trimmings came forth, added their festive touches to the various workspaces. The female staff - office secretaries, administrative assistants, office managers, and so forth - were the more engaged in the process. They put forth and initiated a move to decorate the individual office doors, and set it as a contest whereby the owners of the best so-presented would be awarded a prize.

We four had neither immediate secretarial nor clerical help. Nor did any of us have that womanly touch of class and nicety, so simply enjoyed the various trimmings going up all about. We had no plans to participate, yet felt a bit set aside with our bare office devoid of holiday celebration. The floor personnel knew of our situation, yet began a good-natured kidding about the four old scrooges camped in that dingy office down the hall. We enjoyed the humor of it and took no offense. None had been intended.

The "Moat Dragon," [7] as we affectionately called her, commented on occasion about our situation, and offered assistance of other staff if we wished, including participation in the door contest. We thought it over, and one in our group hatched an idea. After all, we did not want to be known as helpless geeks with no ability whatever to participate in the holiday spirit, further perpetuating the "four scrooges" image. So a plan was devised, set into motion, and in the course of two lunch hours the requisite supplies had been acquired.

We set about decorating that door. It was covered, side to side and floor to ceiling, with an appropriate wrapping paper. A three-inch wide cloth ribbon ran from top center to bottom center, and from left side to right side about two-thirds up from the floor. Affixed to the crossing point of the ribbons sat a large bow of the same material. A suitable holiday greeting, carefully crafted in large lettering on a white envelope, was attached above and to the left of the bow. The whole door took on the appearance of a large box containing a Christmas present. Finally a fair-sized sign was hung beneath the bow, and all was now completed. Our door was decorated, and by our own hands and with our own effort.

It drew quite some attention. Even the door review committee commented thereupon. Our handiwork was entered into the door decoration contest.

What was its appearance?

The wrapping paper was glossy black. Jet black. No pattern. Just plain black. The ribbon was satin, also black, no pattern or

---

[7] A variously affectionate or insulting term, denoting the secretary of the **big** boss: no one dare approach the king without negotiation of permission with the fearsome dragon who patrols his moat.

other decoration. Just plain black. The bow, too, was black, being made of the same ribbon material,

Printed on the exterior of the envelope was a message:

Do not open until Christmas – IS OVER !

The sign, hung below the bow, had a simple message:

BAH !   HUMBUG !

We won a prize!

TV

In their teens our daughters had the chore of doing their nightly homework. One would retire to her room where the daily hubbub of living could be tuned out, and the other would prop herself on the living room floor, in front of the television, scribbling away at her assignments in a multitasking mode, laughing or emoting to her favorite show or two. Mom would be tidying up after the evening meal, and I felt a parental duty to spend some quality time, or at least some time, with the girls. I sat on the sofa, close by the local daughter, and emoted to the shows as well. Lest you conclude that the remote daughter was neglected, be advised: she and I are both radio amateurs and spent much quality time together as well, I being her *Elmer*. [8]

We watched many a show for an hour or two each school evening. *Nick at Night* was her favorite, along with just about every episode of *Daria*, the saga of a high school teenage girl. The episodes seemed to strike so many familiar themes: they rather matched reality in our household to a great extent. For a change of pace episodes of *The Simpsons* filled in.

---

[8] An *Elmer* is a mentor who coached one to acquisition of an amateur radio license, from a nostalgic article detailing its author's mentor, named Elmer.

Periodically, wife and I admonished the local one to turn off the TV set, retire to her room, and do a proper job of homework. This became an item of contention. Mom thought there to be need of undivided attention to the tasks, as did I. But to maintain peace for the short term I intervened, said to let her go for the semester, and when we see her grades suffer, use that as evidence that the TV should be OFF during homework time. But alas! The plan failed. She brought home report cards of A's and B's. What were we to do?

We considered, gave it quit some thought. Perhaps buy a TV for her sister?

ADMIT ONE

R ay was an older chap, a senior member of our research group, in a way our father and confessor. We were an assortment of two senior members, a group of a dozen or so graduate students and a bit of a support staff, associated with a program in the Department of Chemistry. I myself had worked for this same group as an undergraduate, part-time employee, and now had been recruited to come, several years into my engineering profession, to be its research engineer. The group had many electronic systems and needed an engineer to maintain and/or construct these devices.

The position offered partial tuition at the university and I intended to have advantage of it. Unfortunately my undergraduate work, having started out with a reasonable "A" factor, slid downhill as studies continued, and was far less than stellar in the aggregate. I had obtained a Bachelor's degree in Physics, and had converted to Electrical Engineering while employed in the interim period.

My application for admission to the Department of Electrical Engineering as a grad student resulted in a semi-mockingly scolding, the department head saying, "I turn down applicants with a 4.0 factor. Why would I even consider you?

I had already burned my bridges behind me, trusting, as is said, that they would light my way. That episode, however, was rather dark. My true love and wife consoled me, said, "Your degree is in Physics. Why don't you apply at that department?" I was almost ashamed to do so, given my past record as a student and my earlier conversion to Electrical Engineering.

But, two options existing - quit and take employment elsewhere, or apply - I did the latter. By and by a call came to report to a certain professor in the department, and on the visit he counseled me, expressed quite a bit of concern about my poor record, just about dashing all my hopes and dreams, then concluded with, "This department had seen fit to grant you a Bachelor's degree. There is some hope within you. So we shall admit you as a special student with the condition that you complete three graduate courses and maintain a "B" average. If you do so, you may then re-petition for application to graduate school."

He gave me hope, and offered an olive branch, with a challenge. I thanked him deeply and said I would give it my every effort.

I took the first of the eight required courses, one in a field I liked, and completed it with a "B." I was still in the running and had a chance.

Next semester I did likewise, and managed to eke out an "A." This buoyed my spirits: I could even complete the third course with a "C" and yet be in the running. So I realized: one course that had been offered to undergraduate seniors was a mathematics course taught by Physicists. I had taken it my first pass through the senior year and failed! I reasoned: it is a requisite for graduation, so why not take another shot at it, and if I fail, get on with my life. It was difficult. The lot of us worked quite hard at it. And lo! I earned an "A!" This was quite a surprise and further buoyed my spirits.

There was now the further task of applying for formal admission to grad school. The process required presentation of a form letter to three professors who knew me as a student and could vouch for me. I had not been in school for a number of years so knew no such. I asked the young one who taught the math course, and he agreed.

I was also a student of German Literature, although these courses did not count toward a graduate degree. I approached the head of the Department of Modern Languages, my favorite professor in that field, to ask if he might submit a letter on my behalf. He wanted to talk me out of the idea, saying he is not in the field of Physics, but after I explained my situation, he agreed to giver me a high rating, saying it might not do me much good.

I then asked another young professor, who had been assigned to be my mentor in graduate school. But I had not taken any of his courses: he refused, saying he could not vouch for me as a student. This left me crestfallen. I had few if any options open.

My daily preventive maintenance duties took me to one of our laboratories, occupied by Ray. He was a very learned man and also one sensitive to all coworkers. He asked: did my mentor agree to vouch for me? I answered in the negative. He turned about in his chair, then said, "Mike – you disappoint me. Why did you not place one of your form letters on my desk? I expected you would, and I would do my best to assist you."

I expressed thanks, relief, and said I didn't think I could impose on him. But he insisted. I did so. The following morning he said he had forwarded the letter, adding, "I'm new on this campus. Not many people know me. But if some do, you're in." I thanked him profusely.

A few days hence I walked across campus. One of my current physics professors came rather briskly up to me, saying, "Michael! You know Doctor Ray Edwards? How? Oh, by the way – you're in grad school. A board of twenty met to consider new applicants. Yours was on the agenda. Can you believe it! *Ten* did not know who Ray Edwards *was*. The other ten of us set them straight!"

I replied that Ray was a senior researcher on our project. With that he gushed, "He's *here*, on this campus? Could you possibly arrange a meeting where I might meet and talk with him?" Of course I could, and did.

Ray was as a father to us, a benevolent father and wonderful advisor. He had come from the University of Arkansas. I asked where he had obtained his doctorate. We all asked. He always replied it was a small state technical school.

Yes – it was. Massachusetts is a small state. And I found later that Ray, along with our other senior member, had worked together in the past on a little project carrying the name "Manhattan" and had authored hundreds of papers on the subject and many sections of several textbooks as well. I am yet in his debt, and retain his memory fondly.

SERVICE SOON

A guided tour begun several days earlier came to its end and deposited us in Salt Lake City. Our plan had been to rent a car and drive home, the few thousand miles back East. But Murphy once again invoked his infamous law: unexpected duty called. An important meeting had been scheduled, and my presence was demanded at the office ... so my cellphone dutifully reported.

There was insufficient time to complete the original journey, and last-minute air ticketing was far from affordable – with one exception. My travel agent and talented wife, checking options, found a flight from Amarillo to be the lowest cost by far. It fit our change of plan reasonably. Thus off we went, to Amarillo, and to punch off two items from our Bucket List along the way.

There remained two states we had not earlier visited: Kansas and Oklahoma. These, it was decided, would be toured on the way. A mid morning departure gave way to passage into Wyoming, skirting the southern part of its Great Divide Desert, across that imaginary line down the nation that directs rainwater on its western side toward the Pacific, and that on its eastern side, toward the Gulf of Mexico.

This feature affords an interesting means to pass through the Rocky Mountains. Its maximum elevation on our route is about seven thousand feet, and there aren't tall, intimidating mountains to negotiate, no steep, winding passes through which to weave. The mountains we did witness were not towering giants, rather just junior-sized. The general terrain was hilly here and there, and surprisingly flat in many places.

About midday the dashboard's *service engine soon* announcement illuminated. Wonderful! *How* soon, and how far into that high, arid desert would we be goaded until final stranding? And for how long? We nursed our anxiety, asked God for guidance, and plodded forth. Of the few small towns along the road, none seemed to offer much in the line of credible assistance. We simply took our chances, worrying the entire time. Thankfully the ailing mechanical beast delivered us to Laramie by nightfall. We had reached a good-sized city, well east of the Rockies.

We called the rental company. Their instruction? Drive immediately to the nearest airport and exchange autos. The rental firm had an office in town. It was closed, and remained so the following day, the Sabbath.

We sought directions to the airport. It rested a bit to the Northwest, out of town and quite off our planned path. Rental cars? Really, now: it was too small a field to offer much in that department, and what it did, was closed. The *service engine soon* light remained illuminated, naggingly suggesting arrival of doom. We continued, beseeching the Lord for assistance.

The next reasonable option, Fort Collins, Colorado, was approached shortly after noon. Its airport was a twin of Laramie's. The light remained, threatening further as to the auto's condition. Not our original intent, we set our sights on Denver's International Airport, arrived late that afternoon, considerably off our intended route and by then two driving hours' behind schedule. We weaved through dense highway traffic, avoided a major pile-up by guidance of a miraculous angel it would seem, found the airport access roadways, and the rental car area.

The rental agency said they had no autos for a replacement, and to try another large airport. Another large airport? Where might that be? Chicago? Los Angeles? Tokyo? We departed. Although nothing had been done to the auto, the trouble light went dark! Perhaps the bulb simply burned out. Perhaps God had heard our plea. But it ceased being an annoying concern. We simply relaxed, forgot it, and continued on our way.

BURNIBUS

W e continued our road trip. An overnight stop in Eastern Colorado brought us to the gates of Kansas: the Sunflower State. Here and there stood an occasional such plant, not the large variety we had imagined, and those we did see were likely escapees from large farms of same. Perhaps West Kansas is not the area in which they are farmed, or we were past the harvest season. The fields were devoid of them.

Another feature appeared, in small groups at first, then in larger and larger numbers, populating those high windy plains. Windmills. By the score, nay, the hundreds, perhaps thousands. Windfarms engulfed us, ahead, to the left, right, behind, and above. This continued halfway through our journey down the state's West side. Their blades appeared to be at least sixty feet, from hub to tip, possibly a good deal larger.

We entered Garden City, a good-sized metropolis with concomitant fast food establishments, motels, industry, ubiquitous grain elevators, and cattle feedlots about. On its southeast side stood a large industrial yard. What we beheld was most unusual, a marshalling yard for those windmills. Many score of single blades lay in orderly formation, one row following another. A few special trailer trucks stood on the property, just a dolly attached to the far end of a blade while the near end was held by a jig attached to the tractor itself. Also lying in orderly rows, almost as afterthoughts, stood hubs of the mills, the generator pods, and the large single cylindrical stanchions that would support the entire assembly. Yes, Garden City was a garden. No sunflowers. A windfarm garden.

We continued, passing occasional oil wells and cattle ranches. A stop in Oakley, home of Annie of the same fame, sought out some sort of historic marker or information. Aside from a small museum our expectation was not met. So on we drove.

Early evening found us at the next overnight stop, Dodge City. We checked in, then set out for sustenance and to seek what historic markers or evidence might be about. Here expectations were met and well exceeded. The town of old Dodge, a few city blocks long, preserves very well the old west culture, feeling, and air. Monuments, statuary to Wyatt Earp and his companion, Doc Holliday adorned the area, full sized, cast likely in bronze and having stood there for some time, their color being a deep brown patina, tending to black. A monument to a locomotive stood there as well. Yes, old town Dodge was well worth the visit.

Our adventure continued. We "got out of Dodge," southbound. Having been never before in Oklahoma, it was our objective to check off that entry on our bucket list. The countryside was moderately hilly. The route passed more cattle ranches. An occasional oil well pump jack came into view, hopping up and down, then receded into the rear view mirror. We continued a search for sunflowers. None came to view.

The intended terminus of our drive, Amarillo, lay yet South and West. The route took us through western Oklahoma, through that bit of a panhandle separating Kansas from Texas. No large cities or even fair sized towns seem to survive there, just little crossroads, small dots of population every now and then. It was rural. We sped down highways 283 and 56, at the stated limit of 65 miles per hour, Joyce taking a turn to drive that segment.

Michael Toia

Weather was perfect. A sparse few clouds dotted the sky. Temperature was warm, nice, not hot. From the higher spots we could see practically off to Texas and likely beyond. Small brushy plants lined the roads, rather sparsely. There appeared no heavy stands of forest, just an occasional individual tree here and there, and small groves of what I presume could be cottonwoods in the little washes where water might form small streams.

Then we had an unusual experience. A crazy chicken with a vertical tail plume ran from our right, through the bit of brush, and onto the road, not more than fifty feet ahead of us. A roadrunner! By golly, we Easterners had never seen one before, other than perhaps in a zoo, but there it was, a cute little thing, running on the road dead ahead.

Very shortly thereafter occured a "klunk!" I swiveled my head. Joyce checked the mirror. Behind we saw the critter lying flat, rise to its feet again, then keel over – dead, lifeless. It was such a surprise. Our prior education of these had come from cartoons, Wiley Coyote chasing one endlessly out of one desert scene into the next. The cartoons gave Latin-sounding names to the two, Wiley once dubbed "Eternalus Famishus" and the roadrunner "Roadibus Burnibus." We had been led to believe *Burnibus* could run along at least at a hundred miles per hour, likely much more. We were doing but sixty-five.

Alas! A lie! We had been misinformed! It did *not* outpace us at incredible speed. Quite the opposite. We had killed the little darling! Rest in peace, *Burnibus*. We had accomplished the one feat *Famishus* could not. On we drove, a twinge of sadness in our souls.

AMARILLO

A mid July afternoon saw us driving westbound, up in elevation a bit and onto the high plains of West Texas. Destination: Amarillo. Having been there never before, we expected good sized mountains, part of the Rockies, mountain scenes in all directions. What greeted us was quite the opposite, an interesting surprise. The land is flat. Quite flat. Geologically it seems to be a limestone plateau, at an elevation of about 3600 feet. A good guess would say the highest point in town was not much more than a hundred feet above the lowest.

It was an interesting, reasonably sized city, with everything one might desire of a mix of urban and rural life separated by just a few miles. We camped at a motel not far from the airport on the East edge of town, as our few weeks of previous travel were about to come to an end with a flight home, two days hence. Our plan? Enjoy the city a bit, drive about in our rental car, and take in the sights. The unexpectedly level terrain was dotted by numerous small lakes and ponds, many farms and ranches on the outskirts, and a good deal of industry about. As with most towns and cities of the plains states, the ubiquitous grain elevator complex stood tall and proud here and there, sentinels standing guard over the rail lines.

We found an interesting tourist attraction just a few tens of miles to the South, on the East side of Canyon, Texas. There stands *Palo Duro Canyon*, stated to be the second largest in the states, after Grand Canyon. It was large, impressive, beautiful. An obligatory stop at the welcome center and gift shop presented useful tourist information, indicating one may drive to the bottom and back on a loop road a few tens of miles long. We spent an afternoon so exploring, capturing many a snapshot and one or two studio-quality photographs of the multicolored rock formations, then returned to the motel.

Down the highway not a mile stood the Big Texas Steak Ranch, advertising a free steak dinner, with a proviso: It must be eaten in one hour, all of it, all seventy-two ounces: four and a half pounds. I wanted to give it a try, knowing well that the first half-pound would bring me to an absolute halt, and would be willing to pay the establishment's menu price, just for the experience of having been in the place. My more sensible Frau kidded me about it, and laughed me out of it. Drat! An opportunity lost. Most probably for the best. But I shall always wonder …

We dined primarily at nationally-known chain restaurants, and I tell here of an experience at the golden arches, McDonalds, in the northeast part of town. It was a recently opened franchised unit of that famous chain, the vendor of billions and billions of those addictive little sandwiches and French fries. It was quite new. We inquired. It had opened just three weeks earlier.

Here we encountered a shift in paradigm, a good nudge if you will, on ordering procedures. Now the two of us come from the era of Ray Kroc and his meetings with the original McDonald Brothers, their business arrangements, and history whereby this present establishment came to be. Before the nineteen fifties, one could order a hamburger and French fries with a soda in many eateries. The paradigm then was to approach the counter, give the clerk your order, pay for the purchase, and sit down at a table for five to ten or so minutes until your food was prepared and delivered to you, or your order number was called out so you could fetch it from a pickup area.

McDonalds came on the scene in the fifties. The ordering paradigm shifted. It had been at first visit a bit confusing. You stood in line, approaching a counter, deciding what to order. Typically it was a hamburger, French fries, and a soda. As your turn came up, you simply stated your desire, and presto! Your order appeared in front of you in ten seconds or so. The slowest part of the procedure was paying! But citizenry reaching their early teens after 1960 never found this to be unusual, for many *fast food* restaurants had sprung up with the same format of order, pay, deliver, all in one minute or less. As for myself, I had always dreamed of owning an establishment where my largest problem was collecting the customers' money.

We did as we usually had, and approached the counter. The clerk said we had to order first. Why, that's what we were there to do. She directed us backward a bit. There, some five feet or so behind were three rectangular sign board devices, each showing the differing comestibles being offered. But they were more than sign boards. *They were touch screens,* rather huge, about 30 inches across and three feet high. She said we needed to order by touching items on the screen, then approach the counter. Hmmm?

We gazed at one such device. How do we go about ordering? A brush of the hand or finger by accident on a meal item would put it on our order, but it was an accident. We did not want that item. How to erase it? We, both septuagenarians, stood there, two dopes unable to make this thing do our bidding. So help came from the establishment. The fella moping the floor took our order, touched this and that, and in a flash it was done. Our order was in. We thanked him, expressed our ignorance in an apologetic manner, then were asked to the counter where our meal stood, waiting.

Ahh, yes. Times change. One is scant able to keep up. And the sheer embarrassment about this episode is: Carnegie-Mellon University is my Alma Mater, and my dear sweetheart is a former COBOL computer programmer/systems analyst who once worked daily with computers too large to fit into the building housing this restaurant! And we were unable to order at McDonald's. I hang my head in shame.

FARM INN

I n the suburbs of a city sat a very nice, reasonably priced restaurant that enjoyed a large, devoted clientele. Every visit was wonderful, tho always accompanied by a rather long wait to be seated. But the delay was as pleasant, and oft more so, than the meal itself, for reasons I relate as follows.

The proprietors were a family, owners of several acres about the establishment and its parking lot. Their little estate was wonderfully appointed, with well-kept walkways past arrangements of wonderous flower gardens, manicured shrubs, bushes, and a variety of ornamental trees. A stroll thereabout wrapped around a few small ponds teeming with those bright orange, colorful comets that so delight children, and many benches here and there invited one to simply set a spell, rest, enjoy the ambiance, and meditate. The area was a beautiful small park that patrons were encouraged to enjoy while awaiting a table.

Oft on a peasant Sunday afternoon did we visit, check in to obtain our seating time, then take to the promenade. In their seasons the various flowers put on their show, and did so with quite a fanfare. The groundskeepers continually attended to their every need: feeding, watering, weeding, pruning, and all necessary details.   And in the fall, as many of the flowering plants got on to preparing for the coming winter, the carefully selected and previously planted trees and shrubs put on their show of bright yellows, flashing crimsons, intense oranges, purples, and even some interesting blues. We drank it all in, with great appreciation.

Years passed.   The family grew.   Their children had moved away.   Mom and Dad ran the restaurant, but advanced to their senior years.   Likewise the city advanced, marched more deeply into the suburbs, pushed that boundary of rurality out farther from its center, and this line passed by the restaurant.   The latter became a wonderful little oasis in a near suburban, neo-urban high-end neighborhood.   The value of the land rose accordingly, to quite an extent.   Eventually Mom and Dad aged to the point where the body no longer functions as it once did, and realized it was time to retire.   They planned to sell the land and construct therefrom a good-sized nest egg to sustain themselves in their autumn years, and to provide a decent financial estate for the children and grandchildren.

They consulted realtors.   A fairly large housing firm decided they should acquire the property and erect upon it a number of high-end homes.   Mom and Dad negotiated and were in agreement: they would sell their property, assemble their nest egg, and move into retirement.   This plan then became general knowledge.   And with that there rose an outcry of public opinion: it would be unspeakable to destroy such a beautiful park that had offered to so many, so much enjoyment and solitude, for so long.

Petitions were circulated and signed.   Mom and Dad were placed subject to scorn: how could they even conceive of such a dastardly deed?   All this notwithstanding that the park was *private* property, *their* property, owned not by the city, county, nor state, and was hence not a *public* park.   But citizens' pressure prevailed: the local government instituted a taking procedure, to acquire private land for public use, and did so proceed.   Of course the Constitution demands just compensation to the prior owners, but some things are just more just than others.   A hearing was held, a trial by jury conducted, and the jury decided just how much payment was, in fact, just enough to be "just."   I jest not – it was so.

Such a situation is a bit of a kangaroo court. The jurors are taxpayers. Most if not all had enjoyed the park over many years, and their decision, say what one may, was biased – in favor of the government, that government *of* the people, *by* the people, and *for* the people, for they themselves *were* the people. Mom and Dad received "just" compensation – quite less than the development company had agreed to pay. Was it just enough to sustain them in their golden years? I have no idea, as the news media dropped the matter at that point.

So can you see a moral here? There is one. If you own property, and take wonderful care of it, make it a stunningly beautiful garden spot and offer public access thereto, the public will turn on you, eventually take the land from you. So my advice, cruel tho it may be, is not to do so, but rather, to scatter about the property junk cars, old tractors, discarded tires, a junked schoolbus, and let the trees, weeds, vines grow unabated. Render your property as a pubic eyesore. Then, should you wish to sell it to a developer, your neighbors, rather than vilify you, will breathe a good sigh of relief. 'Tiz unfortunate but true.

FORTY-THREE

Nineteen hundred arrived, heralded in a new century. Science had made terrific advances in the previous, the twentieth declared to be the grand century of engineering applications of that knowledge. There remained but a few small items for explanation, and it was assured that that they, too, soon would be *fait accompli*.

Kies had been principle of our high school during my mother's student days, was now retired several years, was quite knowledgeable technically, having been at one time a Physics and Chemistry teacher. He was also a radio amateur, a ham radio operator, first licensed about 1912, and one of our grand science mentors. Sid and I were both young, and newbie radio amateurs.

On a warm June midmorning we paid a visit to Kies. And in his *shack*, as a radio amateur's room is known in the hobby, stood a cabinet displaying various of his mementos gathered over the many years. [9] One was a loving-cup award, a trophy, of silver, on a small walnut stand with quite an inscription upon it. We inquired: and Kies, true to his mentoring style, told the story that I relate below as well as I can recall.

---

[9] The firm *Radio Shack* began historically as a few ham radio stores, later purchased by Tandy.

"The winter of 1924-25 dumped heavy snow in the mountains East of town, in Western Pennsylvania. Roads were impassable for a spell. Even the railroads were stalled here and there, their telegraph lines torn down by the storms. The Pennsy [10] lost a lot of communication. They turned to us, radio hams, to help out, and for a month or two we operated the PREN, the Pennsylvania Railroad Emergency Network. It was our civic duty and, as you know, providing communication in emergencies is a big reason we hams are allowed to exist and use our frequencies.

"About the same time an annual ham radio convention was being planned for the fall of '25, to be held at State College. [11] Our club, the Amateur Transmitters Association – ATA – was asked to do some part of the convention program. I was president."

Kies took a time-out: he had to stoke his pipe. As any friend of a pipe-smoker knows, this is an extended process. Five minutes later, the air now filling with the aroma of his tobacco smoke, he continued:

"Well, we met. Often. We discussed possibilities. *He* suggested we do *that*. *They* talked him down, said we should do *this*. And a few others disagreed with both this *and* that, said we ought do *such-and-such* instead. Why, the process was like trying to herd a zoofull of energetic monkeys. Month after month ticked by. We got no closer to a plan than when we had started. We were probably closer when we did start – many options were still on the table then.

"Time about ran out. We had nothing. So Mac – you know Mac – he and I go back to the nineteen teens together – hatched a plan. We worked together and put on a bit of a show. And we built it around a missing element in the periodic table – Mendeleev's marvel. The table was well known but had a few holes, one at element 43. When you two studied chemistry, it had been found. It's Technetium. But back then it was still missing in action.

---

[10] Pennsylvania Railroad Company

[11] Pennsylvania's State College, located about in the middle of the state in a town of the same name.

"We assembled some radio equipment, five big vacuum tubes sticking out of the top of an oak box, wired to light up and blink from time to time. The thing sat on a wood cabinet like a large podium, with a loudspeaker in the bottom."

Kies stopped a bit. He was a slow, methodical but riveting speaker. He showed us some photos of the device. And his pipe needed restoking. A few minutes later it was up and running again. He continued:

"We developed our convention program, our presentation. A friend and colleague of mine, Herr Doktor Professor Hauschen von Hochschule AusSein was going to visit from Germany to do some new research. He would come to the convention and talk about his work. Element 43, it seems, had just been discovered in old coal mine tunnels as a crystalline carbonate material. The carbonate was a bit unusual. It sublimed [12] at about ten degrees centigrade – fifty degrees Fahrenheit – and when it recrystallized its surface was sensitive to radio waves. It *froze* those waves, capturing them in its solid body. We dubbed it 'Radiocarbonate.'

"The stuff forms as thin coatings on any rocky material. And when you carefully raise its temperature, it goes back to a vapor state, releasing those frozen radio waves. So if it were in a small oven with a coil of wire wound around it and heated very slowly, a radio receiver hooked up to the coil could recover the radio signals. In retrospect, you could think of coating a thin metal or celluloid strip with it and make a sort of forerunner of the tape recorder.

"Now, radio broadcasting had been done for some time right here in the Pittsburgh area, KDKA being on the air with a lot of power for some years. And right nearby, practically under the station, there were many mine tunnels that hadn't been worked in years. When I first heard of Doktor Hauschen's findings, I thought this should be a great spot to look for radiocarbonate. I wrote him and made that suggestion. He was very interested and excited about this possibility, so is coming to continue his research.

---

[12] Vaporized directly from a solid, and re-crystallized as a solid from a vapor.

"Mac and I did a lot of the prep work. Von Hauschen detailed what he needed, and we built it up. The main part was a radio receiver and Mac had one that would do the job. The rest was what you saw in the photos. Its function will be obvious in a bit – just bear with me. All the Doktor had to do was show up and do the demonstration. He gave us instructions of what kind of rock samples to scrounge from mine shafts. Mac went out and gathered a few dozen small pieces."

Kies had to tend his pipe again. Nearby sat a flyer from an electronics surplus store in town, and noontime approached. So Sid and I packed Kies, pipe included, into the car, and we drove off, in search of food, and to pick up a few odds and ends at that store. His story continued to unwind, slowly, during the drive, lunch stop, store visit, and drive back. And that pipe was tended to several times in the interim. He continued:

"A few days before the convention, Mac and I packed everything in his truck. We drove off, to State College, and the next day set about putting it all together on stage. Mac brought along some extra equipment that we thought would come in handy: an Edison cylinder recorder. These were the forerunner of the victrola-type flat records so popular today. [13] He also had a box of cylinders for it. We checked: everything was well set up, in good working order. Since the recorder was not part of the exhibition itself, we set it up backstage in a small room, and ran a pair of wires across the floor from the podium and equipment to it. Mac would sit in the rear to run the thing.

"The convention day broke, a nice sunny, warm day. We expected Doktor Hauschen to arrive mid morning. But the unexpected happened. I got a telegram saying my dear great aunt had suddenly taken ill, was not expected to survive much longer, and asked that I be at her side. She and I were always very close as I grew up: she was the matron of the family. So I had to reluctantly excuse myself, take my leave, and let Mac in charge of the whole thing.

---

[13] C'mon – it was 1959, for gosh sakes, when Kies told this story.

Michael Toia

"Mac met the mid morning train, dropped me off, and picked up Doktor Von Hauschen. I went on my way. Mac took the Doktor to the convention, introduced him around, and at lunch the two of them checked out the display equipment, made sure it worked, tried a sample or two, and made ready for the show to follow lunch. After all, this concept, of freezing and thawing radio waves, was, to say the least, revolutionary news, and got to be the main feature of the convention.

"Well, the show started. Mac introduced Herr Doktor and the topic. Doktor then began, talking about the discovery of element 43 in coal mines, the radiocarbonate, the sublimation, the freezing and release of radio waves, and the fact that many mines in the Pittsburgh area were exposed for five years or more to strong radio waves from station KDKA, this being why he was there to continue his research. He showed a few small rock samples containing the carbonate as a very thin coating not noticeable to anyone in the audience. He put one in the small oven, turned on the equipment. The tubes lit up. Everything started to go into action. No one noticed that Mac had gone to the rear of the stage. He went into the back room to tend the Edison machine.

"The professor, in his heavy accent, explained what he was doing as he went through the steps. He reached a certain point, then said, 'I am told zat a station – KDKA? – ist broadcasting near ver dies roks haf been in ze mine. Wat frequenz ist dat?' A few attendees of the audience shouted back, 'nine hundred twenty kilocycles.' And yes, that's right. In 1925 that's where they were. They didn't switch to today's 1020 kilocycles until 1941.

"Professor Von Hauschen worked the radio receiver, tuned it to that frequency. He turned on the small oven, carefully raised its temperature just as tad. And along with that, Mac, in the back room, had mounted a cylinder on his Edison machine, ready for the action. Some weak sound came out of the loudspeaker, getting a bit stronger, a scratchy sound, lots of noise, but unmistakably some sort of a radio commentator, reading something like the local news. "The crowd exuded a surprised 'ahhh !' It was rather amazing, when you think of it. You should have been in the audience.

"Then someone in the crowd shouted, 'Hey Professor – what's on the ham frequencies?' Doktor Von Hauschen asked what that might be. Several in the crowd shouted back, 'Thirty five hundred kilocycles.' [14] Herr Doktor stroked his beard, looked intently at the radio receiver, said, 'Nah jah – I see how to do zat.' And as he reached toward it, the sound of the recorded broadcast suddenly stopped. In just a bit a new sound came up, again weakly at first, then stronger. It was again just as noisy and scratchy, but clearly it was Morse code.

"The code continued for a few tens of seconds. Suddenly one attendee shot to his feet, shouted, 'That's me! Operating in the PREN last winter!' And a few others shouted agreement: they had been in the same radio net at the same time,

"Well! Pandemonium broke out. Many of the audience rose to their feet, a loud murmuring among them, and they started toward the stage. With that, the Doktor became a bit concerned, loosing control over the presentation, tried to turn off the equipment. The little oven exploded with a light few pops, a bit of smoke blew out of it, and all the apparatus' lights went out. A crowd started to form around Herr Doktor and the podium. Mac, noticing the melee and wanting to protect his Edison machine and cylinders, cut short is recording session, cut loose from the wires, picked up machine and box of cylinders and ran to an adjoining, safe anteroom.

"The gathering mob looked over the demonstration in excited disbelief. One fella, a good friend of mine, looked at the Doktor, in his tux, looked at his shoes. Brown shoes! Who wore brown shoes with as tux? It just wasn't done then. What a breach of protocol. He then looked Herr Doktor right in the eyes, carefully, then attacked, grabbed Doktor's beard and yanked it, yanked it right off his face. And there *I* stood, looking right back into his eyes.

"Discovery! A hoax! And indeed it was. It was exactly as Mac and I had planned, and if I do say so myself, went off rather well. The attacker shouted, 'It's a hoax! This so-called *Doktor*

---

[14] Today we say kilohertz. That didn't come about until 1960.

is just *Kies.*' The mob surrounded me, then rather exuberantly lifted me off my feet, paraded me across the stage, down to the main floor where we had a good, impromptu get-together. Mac came back, and joined us. His *recording* sessions were really *playback* sessions, reproducing the original KDKA broadcast and PREN recording he had made months ago.

"And that's what the loving cup is all about – the best in show for the convention, and the best hoax pulled off at one of those conventions."

* * * * *

That was Keis' story. With a touch of sentiment, he shared the various photos with us, showed us the few of Mac's Edison cylinders, the one with the KDKA broadcast, and the one with the PREN net recording – and a pair, and old pair, of brown shoes, along with a fake beard. And in all it took him five hours and forty-five minutes, consuming a quarter can of pipe tobacco and a box of matches to get it all across to two very entertained and appreciative students of that grand mentor. Thank you Kies, and Mac, and dear friend Sid. You three are now in Aether heaven, and I hope you are yet mindful of me, and putting in a good word for your nostalgic friend. I miss you all.

KP

M any college-bound young men sign up for Reserve Officers' Training Corps classes. Various schools of higher learning host such, be they Army, Navy, Air Force, or other programs nationwide to train service-bound *cadets*. The program teaches military procedure, drill, techniques, and the use, care, and maintenance of warfare hardware. To many it is a reward in itself. Navy cadets get a chance to go to sea for a summer training stint, or go on to NavAir and learn to fly. Air Force counterparts get similar training about air operations, and many also learn to fly. Army cadets become more "ground pounders." Such was my fate.

Our university offered two Army ROTC options: Corps of Engineers and Signal Corps. We geek-like radio amateurs clustered to the latter, learning what we could about military field communications, techniques, equipment, and procedures. At the end of the sophomore year we were conscripted to a summer of training, off to Fort Gordon, GA. It was our "boot camp," with all its nuances and effects. My first meal on arrival was also my sole experience with that military epicurean comestible known as "S O S." The first mouthful surprised, overwhelmed my taste buds and tongue. It was, in a word – *awful*. But I was hungry, so forced myself to finish it. Seconds were offered but declined. S O S is everything a military person says it is, and a great deal less.

Boot camp was interesting. There were forced marches at unannounced times, a night compass course to be negotiated through a swamp, training on signal equipment in the field to be set up, moved, and struck most any time. I became rather proficient at driving anchor stakes into the ground to support tactical quick-up radio masts, first during daylight hours, then at two in the morning by the light of a military flashlight. There was also the laying of field telephone wire and cable and its retrieval onto large, hand-cranked reels.

Other miscellaneous duties were assigned. Guard duty. Grounds policing – cleaning up and removing all foreign objects that could indicate some human activity had been in the area, a tipoff to a potential enemy in an actual war-type situation. And there was also KP – kitchen Police – to help the cooks put out every meal. I found these to be a spell of very long days but a means to eat well, never a meal to miss.

One occasion had our company in the field for several days. In that time I was assigned to KP for a twenty-four hour spell. The day's meals were to be "C-Ration." The Army had piles of this stuff in warehouses, aging, and was bent on disposal of as much as possible. Now if you were military at the time, you recall that a *ration* would feed one soldier for a day. It included a few "C" units, each a single serving tin can and a "P-38" folding can opener hunters and hikers can acquire to this day. I have about a dozen scattered about the house, and one in my wallet.

A "C" unit contained varieties of meat-protein rich food, such as tuna and noodles, beans and wieners, ham and potatoes, corned beef hash, turkey in gravy … and *pork sausage patties*. This unit, when opened without heating, revealed a slug of solid lard in which were encased several hamburger-shaped pork sausages, the latter having the consistency and taste of very greasy sawdust. Of the lot, many troops considered this particular "C" unit to be inedible.

The mess line was set up. Troops assembled and filed by, to pick up a ration box. Some opened their box, looked inside, began removing the less desirable "C" units, and exchanged them for more desirable ones from other boxes. This left the disgusting stuff to the troops at the end of the line. The cooks witnessed this activity, informed the company commander. The latter issued an order: all "C" units were to be returned to the mess area at once.

The cooks brought out a few large field soup pots, ordered the KPs to open all those cans, and dump their contents – all of them – into the pots. About two hundred and fifty were so disposed. We became quite adept at just how to flick the wrist with that P-38 opener and get the job done quickly. To this day I yet retain that skill.

We finished. The cooks set up field burner units, similar to the Coleman gasoline-fueled single burner camping stoves but considerably larger, one for each pot. The "stew" came up to temperature. It was an unappetizing. repulsive-looking sea of beans, wieners, chunks of tuna, noodles, bits of ham, potatoes, those pork sausage patties, some now-heated and perhaps digestible lard, and assorted other possibly edible stuff.

The company was again ordered to the mess line, now with mess kits at the ready. Troops approached the pots. KPs ladled a good dollop of that swill into their kits. I'd say less than half of the company contingent came to lunch that day, and made do with the other components of their ration box.

We KPs stood there, ladling away, dollop after dollop of hog slop. But strangely, the odor was not bad. It was rather somewhat enticing. So as the last of the line trooped by, the pots but a third empty, our turn came. With a bit of trepidation, dispelled by a considerable helping of hunger, I screwed up my courage, dolloped a small bit into my mess kit and sampled it.

Wow! It was *good*! Other KPs on duty did the same. And in just a short while many of us had consumed about as much *C-ration stew* as our stomach capacity could handle.

Yes, KP duty meant a very long day. But one ate well. One did that day. In fact, several did.

PUMPKIN

F all arrived on time, per its usual schedule. Football weather set in. Overnight temperatures fell. Maples, hickories, sassafras and others traded their lush green for a wonderful display of artwork: flaming oranges and reds, yellows, rusty browns. The ginkgos in particular put on quite a show that year, a beautiful, dazzlingly golden yellow that, in the bright Indian Summer sunlight, threw over the entire area an incandescence of radiant beauty. They appeared to be afire. Late October approached.

Our development, being new, had that year acquired a handful of homes and families. We observed a number of young children playing in the area, and recalled our youth, the custom of dressing in costumes, calling on households on Halloween, garnering our small sackfulls of candy and treats. Though we were now older, our grown children having moved on to start their families, the thought of the little ones ringing our bell, exclaiming "Trick or Treat!" cast the season's mood upon us. My dear spouse had set in a decent supply of treats to hand out on the anticipated evening.

From a short trip to town we returned home one mid afternoon, saw our house sitting up on a small rise near the end of the neighborhood, the highest point of the development, commanding a prominent position. Not an extravagant structure, nonetheless it rested there in a sort of semi-elegance, as if satisfied to be so situated and to be rather eye-catching. We approached. Meine Frau spoke. "There's something missing." A few of the neighbors had some seasonal decorations about, a sheaf of dry cornstalks about the mailbox post, a bale or two of straw with stuffed mannequin-like figures, imitation spiderweb material here and there. Our home had none. She thought we should do at least some little decorating.

A day or two later, and a few before Halloween we again went atown for a bit of lunch, to mail some letters, to purchase a few odds and ends. A local mower repair and sales shop had set up a pumpkin patch maze in front of the store, to the delight of area small children and parents. And at the nearby small mall we were again awestruck by the ginkgos, their having acquired that amazing, glowing golden yellow coloration, and so enjoyed the sight. The shops and stores had put out some Halloween displays here and there. The market had a large assortment of pumpkins prominently displayed near its entranceway. Wife exclaimed, "That's what's missing! A pumpkin! I'll buy a pumpkin and set it out by our front porch, where the neighborhood kiddies will see it, know we are likely 'open' for Halloween treats. It will be the perfect touch."

I, on the other hand, know little to nothing about how to decorate, neither inside nor out, have no eye for the process, no imagination as to what small touches would improve an existing scene, so let it entirely up to her. She directed me to the market, to drop her off. She would go in, buy a pumpkin, and return in a minute. I should just park the car nearby, watch for her, and come by to pick her up in a wee bit. With the drop-off accomplished, the radio provided entertainment as I waited. She wasn't to be long. But tarry a bit she did. Not a problem. Anytime she goes to market she recalls we need this and that, and even a short stop ofttimes becomes a mini shopping trip. But at last she reappeared, pushing a shopping cart with four bags in it. I drove to the pickup point. We opened the hatchback. I saw the cart, the bags. No pumpkin. I questioned: "There's a pumpkin in here? Some assembly required?" Perhaps its pieces were within the bags.

Michael Toia

It was not so. The bags loaded, she pushed the cart back to the storefront, and, with receipt for same in hand, picked out a pumpkin. A store employee loaded it into the car. And she was so right: it did set off the house nicely, sitting atop that small knoll, observing its surroundings

ARMS ROOM

The Army has its specific rules, regulations, and procedures. One involves what was known as the "Officer of the Day." I relate the "when, where, why, what, how, and who" of that position from the viewpoint of a two-year commitment to the service of our country.

An Army *Company* consisted of somewhat over two hundred troops under command of a Captain. It was organized generally into a handful of platoons, each commanded by junior officers, Lieutenants, with subservient Lieutenants and NCOs tending to other specific matters within the platoon. Each day one of the Lieutenants was appointed as "Officer of the Day," or OD. He was assigned additional duties to his usual list.

Officers were required to pay a nominal fee for their meals when they ate at the company mess, but could choose to go elsewhere should they desire. The OD, by orders, was required to take his meals at the company mess hall. In fact, he was required to be the first in line at each of the day's meals, take a very small portion of everything on the menu, sample it, approve of the menu, then declare the mess open for the troops. He then took coffee, sat in the officers' area. No officer, the OD included, was permitted to take his full meal until the last of the troops had been called to mess. As a reward, the OD's meal was free.

The company also had weapons. In ours each man was assigned a rifle. Several officers were assigned pistols. We had some heavier weapons: a few machine guns, a few mortars, grenades, ammunition and so forth. One of the OD's daily duties was to conduct an inspection of the arms room, do a complete inventory of the company's assigned weaponry, and sign a certificate of same. He could schedule the inspection at his choice of time. Some did it immediately after reveille formation, some toward the end of the day, and others at intermediate times.

During one such duty, I instructed the company armorer – the trooper in charge of the arms room – to standby for inspection at 0930 hours. Mess inspection was due at 1130 and I knew I could be done in time.

At 0910, he approached me with bad news: he had locked the keys inside the arms room! I asked where there was a spare set. There wasn't.

Together we walked to the arms room. It was in one of those WWII temporary wooden barracks type buildings, so characteristically painted a pale yellow as were the thousands of its cousins. The door was closed, and three horizontal pieces of 3"x 3" heavy angle iron spanned its expanse, top, center, and bottom. These were slotted at their ends, through which large eye bolts, attached very securely to the door frame, protruded. A heavy padlock on each eye bolt assured that the angle iron could not be removed.

We walked around the building. The arms room was an interior room. Internally its walls were covered with a netting of chain link fence material. It would be very difficult to attempt entry other than through its door. After a bit of study, I ordered the armorer to the supply room, to bring back a heavy claw hammer, a nail bar, and a crowbar. He did so.

We began investigating the door frame. The nail bar could begin a penetration, and the frame began to yield to our attack. A gap opened a bit, and the crowbar could then find entrance. We worked together, and in about twenty minutes had the entire door frame, complete with door, eyebolts, angle iron and locks, standing across the hallway as a single assembly, leaning against the wall. We completed the inspection, in time for mess inspection. I instructed the armorer to stand guard, completed my mess inspection, and ordered the first troop who had finished lunch to guard duty as relief for the armorer so the latter could get his lunch.

I sat at the officers' table, related an interesting tale. The company commander said, "You did *what!*" He ordered me to accompany him to the arms room, and several other junior and noncommissioned officers tagged along. There was quite a commotion as we entered the area, a good deal of raucous laughter, comments of disbelief, some of what this junior Lieutenant had done, and what he was in for.

The Captain was hardly amused. Quite the contrary. He brought me up on charges. I had destroyed government property. The next morning the battalion had a short hearing on the matter. The Captain said he thought a court-martial was in order, but acknowledged that I was a reasonable junior officer. However, government property had been destroyed.

I was given an opportunity to defend my actions. Here's the defense:

* * * * *

"Sir! I was the duly appointed Officer of the Day. My orders were to inspect the arms room. I had chosen to do so at 0930, allowing ample time to perform my mess hall inspection duty. I ordered the armorer to standby for inspection at the appointed time.

"The armorer approached me, stated that he had by accident locked the keys to the room inside same, and advised that there existed no spare set of keys.

"I ordered him to the supply room to obtain one claw hammer, one nail bar, and one crowbar. He did so. We two began removal of the door frame at approximately 0945, and by 1005 had the frame, door, and all its security appurtenances detached from the room, resting as a single unit, leaning against the wall opposite the arms room.

"I completed my inspection as ordered. There was no dereliction of duty in that regard.

"I completed in time to tend to my duty as mess hall inspector. There was no dereliction of duty in that regard.

"As to the charge of destruction of government property: the property was not destroyed. It was kept intact, as a single unit, ready for a carpenter to re-install it. In the process the armorer and I recovered the errant keys. Then I went to lunch.

"I maintain the following: If a junior officer, a recent ROTC graduate Second Lieutenant, a somewhat disparagingly termed 'ninety day wonder' is able, with naught but a hammer, nailbar, crowbar, and one assistant, penetrate the arms room in less than twenty minutes, I maintain that, Sir, there is a security problem on this post. I claim that, by my actions, I have rendered to you a valuable service and request dismissal of charges of destruction of government property."

* * * * *

The battalion commander considered this plea. He rubbed his chin. He knew that all battalion arms rooms are similarly protected. He saw my point, and ordered charges dismissed. But, just a bit amused, he approached me as I stood at strict attention, looked me directly in the eyes, and asked:

"You did that in twenty minutes? How was that possible?"

I replied, "Sir: I was hungry."

OUR PET

"To a dog, you are family. To a cat, you are staff," as was well said by Paul Harvey on one of his radio shows. Years ago and but a few months after we married, my bride asked pensively, "Could we get a pet?" My first reaction was that she wanted a cat. I have nothing against cats, and for that matter had two of them as a child. The first ran off. The second proved to be such a "mouser" that its fame spread throughout the area. We lived in a second-story apartment and Mom, out of respect for the landlord, said we could not keep it there. Granddad's house was its first home, and we visited frequently.

Kitty gained weight. He became *fat*. Mom complained to granddad: he was overfeeding it. Granddad said he gave it a saucer of milk a few times a week, and fed it about twice a week. But a few months more and kitty lost weight. He became a sack of bones!

The house, mouse infested, went to mouse free in four months. My pet was a mouser! Its fame spread through the neighborhood. It was loaned to a friend, with the same result as previously. Kitty got fat, then lost weight, and the house repeated the condition change as had granddad's. Kitty was loaned out again. After two more I lost track of my little pet.

But she wanted a dog.

A dog? Wow! I've always loved dogs, and had one as a teenager. It disappeared one day, I was told the result of a traffic accident. I did miss him. And a dog? Hmmm – I could go for that. Shortly after we acquired our first of a line of dogs, a little puppy from the pet department of "Atlantic Superama." The Superama was like today's Wal-Mart Superstore, on steroids. They sold everything. Groceries. Appliances. Cars. Caskets. And pets. We parted with $5.00 and departed with a wonderful little friend, our first dog.

Fast forward now about four decades. We've since housed six dogs, loved them to the end. And our fifth and wonderful Belgian Sheep dog, Pepper, departed one day after fifteen years of loving companionship. She had been such a blessing to our two little girls, protective and gentle to a fault. But as the girls grew to their teens, Pepper did the same, and sadly the end came. She expired on the front porch one spring afternoon.

We mourned the loss for a bit. A few months later we decided: it was time for another pet. The family discussed what we would want. An English Sheep dog? A German Shepherd? A Lab? The whole family set its sites on acquisition of dog #6. We checked shelters. Pet stores. Newspaper ads.

One day, on a drive to Pittsburgh we stopped for supplies and groceries for a short stay at our Laurel Highlands summer cabin. Wife went to the market. Daughters and I walked along the tiny mall. And lo! There was something new. A pet store!

Its tractor-beam towed us in, "just to look." Resistance was futile. We saw fish. We saw kittens. And we saw – puppies! We looked. Puppies looked back. Mutts, of course. Just $59.95. But all our dogs had been mutts. The girls got mom, lured her to the tractor beam. She was towed in. She looked. The puppies looked back. We pondered. But we were on our way outbound. It wasn't quite the time to buy.

We spent the night at the cabin, and departed the next morning. In Pittsburgh we scanned the newspapers, looking for dogs. We visited more pet stores, arrived at no decision, other than: if a particular puppy at the Highlands store was still there, we would buy her for our next pet.

The return found us retracing our outbound path, to the Laurel Highlands, to the pet store. Our choice of puppy was still there – and on sale! She was the "manager's special," marked down to $29.95. How could we resist? She was brought out for closer inspection. We were warned: "This one needs a lot of love, but gives a lot of it back, too. If you can't cope with that, don't take her." We could. We did. We left. $29.95 [15] poorer, one puppy richer.

To match her coloring and overall activity, she was christened "Ginger." She had been billed as a type of collie, but developed instead into a terrier. *Terror* was actually the more appropriate term, particularly outdoors. Mom took her to obedience school. It was a waste of money. Younger daughter bought a home video course on dog training. Another waste of money. The loveable mutt didn't take to training: *she* trained *us*.

Ginger was our pet for fifteen years. She had the affection and dependence a dog owner craves. She did, indeed, need a lot of love but returned a lot, as was advertised. Had you met her, you would have loved her too. But alas! The end came. She, too, died on our front porch, almost exactly where Pepper left us for the last time. We miss her. We miss her deeply.

Her ashes are now under a lovely dogwood tree out in the yard. I call it the "Ginger tree." As I mow the lawn, I always talk a bit to her when near that tree. I guess I'm just a sentimental old geezer now, but it gives me some solace.

---

[15] Plus tax.

Rest in peace, Ginger. And Pepper, Becky, Midgen, Cracker, Duchess, pets # 6, 5, 4, 3, 2, and 1. You all have brought us so much love and companionship through our life. We shall never forget any of you.

INSPIRATION

F rom whence flow the ideas, the themes of a story or literary work? Possibly and likely there are various sources, springs, fountains. It's oft said to write, rely on your own experiences: take your cue from life itself. This requires attention to detail, a memory, facility with a vocabulary, and a personal dictionary, if you will, of familiar and readily available words, phrases and constructs. And as to experiences, we aged have a great advantage over the youth: we've lived a fantasmagoria of them, many predating the birth of the latter. And when your manuscript is completed according to this formula, it will most likely be a fictitious reality, a mix of the true that an historian can uncover, and the make-believe that he cannot.

Consider the genesis of a story line. A particular sequence of possibilities wells forth in the mind. Fleeting reminisces come and go. I find it convenient to carry a notepad at all times and record a single sentence, perhaps a phrase, a few words that, when later consulted will, in an instant, refocus thought on that particular episode of past life, thereby erecting a very basic skeletal structure, a scaffold, on which a story might be constructed.

As an example, the simple phrase *"CRUISE SHIP CASINO"* later flushed my memory, my fading memory, of a rather humorous anecdote three decades earlier, concerning my spouse, my gal, my love, salivating over an unexpected windfall, a fifty-dollar slot machine payout. She turned to exit the casino, headed to the gift shop. The humor lies in the detail of how that desire was successfully arrested. That story, *CASINO*, appears in my work, *FROG TONGUES and other Recollections of an Old Patriarch.* [16]

This may seem to be a crass exhibition of self-aggrandizement, but amply demonstrates my point. And that point is: I have had a most recent experience, the scaffold on which *this* story is constructed. For, over several years, my daughters had asked that I put in writing various tales I had related to them as they grew from the age of continuous recall to that of leaving the family nest, launched into their own adult lives. I had done so. At first there were fifteen. Then it grew to thirty, forty-five, sixty, and for some reason continued. The process went on for a decade. Meantime the girls married and advanced to their mid thirties.

My gal then inquired: how many of these stories had I captured and passed on to our daughters, recorded as texts on a sequence of CDs? She asked that I compose those into a manuscript, and she would send it off to a publisher, sometimes not reverently called a *vanity press*, and have the thing produced as a book. This was to be my Christmas present. And the recent experience, about which I here write, is the appearance of that book at our doorstep in a FedEx envelope. As the eight month process from completion of manuscript to printed book, working with the people at Dorrance Publishing, passed by, the endeavor entered into discussion at the office from time to time, as well as among social contacts. There developed thereby a small but devoted set of *groupies* – all interested in my evolving experience, many desiring to dig out that book lurking within their souls and follow a similar process.

To that end almost all have inquired: how does one go about writing a book: how was *I* doing it? It was an interesting question,

---

[16] Dorrance Publishing, 2016, ISBN 978-1-4809-3214-2

Michael Toia

the immediate answer to which was what we all were taught years ago: write what you know about. And this itself, this question, settled into my mind: From whence come the ideas, the themes of a story or literary work? And an answer, slowly, over the many months of setting about completing *FROG TONGUES*, slowly formed. Write about your own experiences. But *HOW*? And that latter question answered *itself*.

It's said that, as one dies, one's life flashes before oneself. So the trick I find is to die – to die slowly – sufficiently slowly that each such flash can be captured, dumped into a word processor, and set into more permanent form. So my advice: fear not death. It is inescapable. It will come. Welcome it, nurture it. We all die one day at a time. And as those daily flashes occur, be ready: record them on a notepad that you carry about, or on a personal voice recorder carried in your pocket. Then take those little memory-jogging phrases to your quiet little home corner, and begin erecting your story on their skeletal scaffold. Add details that you remember. Fill in those you cannot recall completely. Employ amply both poetic and literary license. The story line will evolve, part true, part fiction: you are writing neither a technical manual nor a scientific report. Fiction is permitted.

Follow these, my personal three guiding principles:

1   Never let the truth get in the way of a good story. [17]
2   If it ain't the truth, it shoulda been. [18]
3   That's my story, and I'm stickin' to it.

Don't get complicated. Many details of those past life flashes will be fuzzy, erroneous. My gal, my sweet wife of many decades, will read my first drafts, say, "That's not the way *I* remember it. Where did you come up with this?" Fuzz it a bit. It's a story. Factual details are not critical.   Who cares that the river by my home town, the Allegheny, becomes rendered as the Algosonkin, or, for that matter, any other name? Nobody really important to the story itself or to its enjoyment will.

---

[17] Attribution to Mark Twain
[18] Old Texas saying

Do not use living persons' actual names without permission. You might honor deceased friends by using their names. Add details to augment what you do recall. Invent what you cannot. Put it all in a cohesive whole that will be entertaining and/or instructive.

And above all, have fun in so doing. If you find your most amused audience consists of but one person, and that person is yourself, so what? But do share your work with close friends. If *they* see humor, instruction, utility, or something useful in your writing, then you may be on to something. But you've had fun to this point, and have achieved a goal, scratched an internal itch, so to speak, and have something your grandchildren will likely enjoy years hence.

TERRORISTS

O ne wonders what goes on in the minds of government officials. They take an oath of office, vowing to defend the Constitution against all enemies, foreign and domestic, then act though they have never *read* the document, much less memorized its salient features. They consider that oath as naught but a simple check-off on a list of otherwise useless administrative details and formalities in ascent to their higher position.

I am particularly incensed that a former Secretary of Homeland Security, one Janet Napolitano, has cast aspersions against my wife. That meek, sweet woman that stays on as my spouse, easygoing almost to a fault, is a genuine American woman. Loving, beautiful, generous, a fantastic mother to two now-grown young ladies, and patriotic to the United States, as am I. A devout Christian, careful shopper, good with management of our resources, she is just an all-around wonderful woman and wife. To seek one better would is but a fool's errand. None exists.

She and I attend Church on Sunday, then customarily eat out at a nice restaurant, and likely then stop by Wal-Mart where she acquires the week's groceries. One notices her wheeling a shopping cart or two to the car, stashing in the weekly purchases. Some items ... toilet paper, paper towels, perhaps a new blanket or so ... are bulky, suggesting the illusion of a food hoarder.

At Wal-Mart there will be a stop by the sporting goods desk, inquiry about ammunition for our small arrangement of rifles and pistols. We like to keep in practice at the range, and will easily burn off a hundred rounds per hour at an evening of practice. After all, we are firm believers in gun control. If one is to own a gun, one need be quite adept at its control, this best brought about by continuous practice.

Alas, Wal-Mart is almost universally devoid of small arms ammunition. We feel like Mother Hubbard trying to find her poor dog a bone. When some exists, my sweet Joyce will purchase about one to two hundred rounds for planned practice. And because of the likes of Napolitano, it will be a cash purchase, lest there be a paper trail that "Big Brother" will inevitably follow. 'Tiz sad that we have grown to distrust our elected and appointed overseers, a paranoia that unfortunately is daily becoming more and more well-founded. We trust our government about as far as it trusts us, and that ain't very.

Why has ammunition supply dried up so? Could it be that Homeland Security has purchased, and continues to do so, *billions* of rounds of small arms ammunition? Billions? For what purpose? Why, with 300 million of us in the country, they have about ten rounds to dispatch each and every one. Am I Paranoid? Maybe. Maybe not. You judge.

Now Janet has declared these Bible-thumping, food-hoarding Christians who cling to their guns to be *incipient terrorists*. Indeed. It is because of this tomfoolery of a statement that my meek, "I want no trouble" spouse has recently studied, taken and passed a test, thereby allowing her to obtain a concealed carry permit in our state, which she now holds, proudly, along with her newly-acquired NRA membership card, her Smith and Wesson M&P .22 semi auto, and purse-sized Sig P280 semi auto.

Yes, Janet – you think of us as possible terrorists. And, you just may be right. Just try to usurp the Constitution. That second amendment is there for a very good reason. Our founding fathers tried to throw off an oppressive government, and found it necessary to resort to force of arms to do so. I pray that *not* become necessary again. Wake up, Janet. Consider what you are doing. Read the Constitution. Read your oath of office, where you swore to defend it against all enemies, foreign and domestic. Note carefully the term *domestic*. You swore to bear true faith and allegiance to same, and took that oath without mental reservation or purpose of evasion – as did my sweet spouse and I, when we, too, took office as employees of the government. The difference is we stand by our oath. Not to do so is known as perjury.

Box in an otherwise peaceful bear and it can strike out. Whether you please or not, we shall keep our Constitutional claws sharp. And our powder dry.

PROPHECY

E arth's citizenry know the biblical story of Jesus, His lowly
birth, His bed, that of hay, on a manger in a stable among the
livestock, taught as God instructing earthlings: wealth and
expensive trappings are unimportant. The event had been
prophesized ages in advance, to wit: as the time drew nigh, a star,
the famed star of Bethlehem, appeared in the sky, seen far and wide
by various persons familiar with the prophecy. In particular, we are
told, wise men from the East observed it, followed it, night after
night, and traveled day after day in the same direction. They were
so led to the very bedside of the Holy Child.

This advent story speaks of three wise men, three kings of the
Orient ... China? ... traveling from far to the East, bearing gifts of
gold, frankincense, and myrrh. Arriving at the manger scene, the
trio praised the Child, presented their gifts, then departed to return
from whence they had come. We loose contact with the party here:
the Bible appears not to further comment upon them. And it is this
trio, these generous three, that seemingly had by their visit, ignited
another prophecy. But I outpace myself ...

I muse: this biblical account gave rise to the custom of exchanging presents each Christmas, the anniversary of Jesus' birth.

That custom, the gift-giving, has developed into a near frenzied activity, commencing a bit after start of school every fall, on to Christmas day and through the after-Christmas sales. Today every merchantable item, almost exception-less, carries a simple message: *hecho en China*. Very little in the gift department is made in America, the lion's share coming as indicated by that simple phrase.

Why, just recently I had an inexpensive tire pump that, I hold to be true to its creator's intent, inexplicably, irretrievably, unexpectedly and disgustingly, self-annihilated as I endeavored to obtain a good, firm filling in my bicycle tires. It was not repairable. *It* was made in China. Thus a mission was initiated: go to town and buy a quality tire pump not of Chinese manufacture.

The local Lowes sold two types of pumps. *Hecho en China*. Advanced Auto Parts had a few different types, from a standard hand pump to an electrically driven one. Again all Chinese. Two other auto parts stores visited revealed the same characteristic. Wal-Mart was not an exception, nor was Ace hardware. A tire pump not made in China existed not in our locale, certified by an intensive, two day thorough search. Apparently no one but the Chinese now posses tooling, materials, designs, technology, and expertise necessary for the manufacture of bicycle tire pumps. And this seems to hold for merchandise in general. If it's not from China, it tends to be occasionally from Mexico, but generally from the Orient

It occurred to me that those three kings foresaw this, and had set it into motion, they being harbinger prophets of same. *They* saw that, by this act, this prophecy fulfilled and cast into a new, presaging light, would one day profit their countrymen. China would become the world center of manufacturing and purveying all sorts of goods needed to meet the demands of their prophecy, this innate requirement to give gifts at Christmas.

And to corner the world market for bicycle tire pumps. A pity, really ...

Michael Toia

BAGLESS

S ummer ushered in Fall. Climate moderated. My love set her sights on yet one more visit to her favorite town: Las Vegas. And on a Sunday afternoon off we went, a drive to the airport, a five hour flight, and into Nevada about ten PM local time, but ... one of our bags went AWOL. An hour's delay attempting to procure the prodigal parcel netted naught but a copy of a missing bag form. It will be delivered to our hotel – so we were informed,

Off then, to rental cars, to a long queue, four agents servicing the crowd. Critical thinking suggested we were witness to an historic event: composition of the very first draft of an auto rental contract, requiring major rewrites for each hopeful standing on line. I tended what luggage we had received. Wife stood on line. At last she was next. And as we watched, somewhat incredulously, somewhat amusingly, but downright annoyingly, agent #4 went off duty, followed in immediate succession by her fellow agents 3 and 2, a changing of the guard apparently. It seemed the gods of travel were up to mischief that night. Midnight arrived, reluctantly dragging Monday morning along.

In a bit more than an hour, it was our turn. And in somewhat short order we had a contract, headed for the rental car line, and were at last on wheels. Just one checkout lane was active, with one auto blocking us, occupied by a person that must never before have rented a car, this being her first confusing time. Another wait of fifteen minutes, and we arrived at the starting gate. We were off! Into the confusing jumble of roads, well past one AM, with a drive of yet an hour and a half to go – to Pahrump.

A 2:40 arrival got us into a rental cottage unit, a lovely little space, comfortable, and immediately off to bed, the alarm set for five-thirty: we had an engagement at 7 on a firearms range three quarter's hour distant. And faithfully did the alarm performed its assigned duty, emitted an awful stream of noises, woke us. A quick breakfast of a banana and a few fig newtons – all the food at that moment and place available – accompanying a cup of complimentary coffee made by the cottage's provided brewer, got us up and running. An incoming cellphone call reported that our wayward luggage was yet at the originating airport, and will be put on a flight tomorrow, Tuesday. We were without toiletries, clean underwear, toothbrush, etc., and survived as best we could.

Not long after arrival at the firearms institute, in time to draw our rental equipment, pick up the requisite six hundred rounds of 9 mm ammo, we commenced classroom and range work: 8 AM till 1 PM. A box lunch in the lecture hall while attending lectures on firearms handling, safety, laws, gave way to 2:30, and a return to the firing line for yet more instruction, and firing on command with differing disciplines from various distances.

5:30 PM heralded the end of day 1. Monday's work was complete.

Evening found us at Wal-Mart, acquiring underwear, toothbrushes, etc. to replace the contents of the wayward bag. The range schedule continued the second day, a total of sixteen hours of defensive handgun hands-on coursework, box lunches at noon during further lectures on safety, law, hearing protection, and gun related matters. A bit more telephone chatter with the airlines indicated our bag would arrive on flight 822 at 7:20 PM that evening, Tuesday

On completing the day's range work we drove, back to LAS, met the flight, searched for the wayward parcel, searched for an hour and a half: no bag. Apparently the prospect of travel frightened the poor thing. It stubbornly and shyly remained at our originating airport, hiding from sight. A night drive back to Pahrump delayed bedtime until midnight. Now we could relax, one hundred forty additional miles on the rental car, range training complete. We awoke Wednesday, at a more leisurely time and rate.

Sans bag.

Our appointment next was with the county Sheriff. Wife called information, asked for the Sheriff's number. She called the number provided. And got Sheri's Ranch. Sheri's? Wrong number. A second try got through.

An unhurried breakfast and ten AM checkout was easily met. Information provided by the staff led us directly to the Sheriff's office. Wife mentioned the wrong number call, to Sheri's, and was told they have a really good lunch. We were instructed as to how to find the place. A bit of paperwork and photography netted our State of Nevada Concealed Weapon Permits. [19] They were now in hand, this being the initial purpose of our travel.

Due in Vegas later that day, we spent time looking over Pahrump, a small desert city, with most all of the amenities one could seek in a hometown. The thought occurred that retirement there could actually be rather pleasant, the firearms academy and its ranges nearby being an attraction.

We drove about, found Homestead Road, traveled it Westbound to Sheri's at the end of the pavement near the California line. We and noon arrived, so decided to try their fare. Sheri's was on the left. Lo! It is a brothel, and world-renown. But the building was quite upscale and the grounds nicely appointed. We entered, found a place to sit, and ordered lunch. It was, indeed, well enjoyed, good food, friendly service, and occasional views of the lady staff in working attire, a nice touch. The gift shop yielded

---

[19] Permission to carry a concealed firearm.

a few souvenir items, and off we went, to Sin City, the sixty or so miles to the Southeast.

Yes, we went to Sheri's. Sheri's Brothel. Got the tee shirt. And a coffee mug.

On entering our hotel, we spied two friends having their lunch, their presence being the second reason for the trip. There sat the widow of one of my two best friends – I am fortunate to be married to the other – and the widow's younger sister companion. We greeted, hugged, then went to the check-in desk for an efficient process, and shortly thereafter basked in the comfort of a well-appointed room. A call to the bell desk, inquiring of the missing bag, was profitless. We continued to make do with the bit of emergency undies and toiletries acquired Monday at Pahrump's Wal-Mart.

The evening was pleasant indeed. Our foursome attended dinner theater in Oldtown, a twinge off Freemont Street. Cuisine was good, not outstanding, but worth the price. The show was interesting and engaging, tho about ten times or more too loud. Electronic amplification, nowadays massively abused in the entertainment industry, blared its raucous noise, possibly in an attempt to mask the operation of the jet engine test stand down the hall. It succeeded at it as well. As a professional engineer by education and trade, I took a mental note to examine the engine facility on my next visit, its being apparently so close. Such devices interest me.

A Thursday AM call to the bell desk confirmed the continued absence of the wayward travel bag. We four enjoyed a nice breakfast. The sisters decided to retire to their room and go their separate way that morning. My sweets and I did the same, reconnoitered the adjoining Fashion Place mall. Lunch was attended at the food court, where pizza was surprisingly well above average fare. Wife enjoyed some window shopping. We returned to the hotel, relaxed the remainder of the afternoon. Later, joining the other two, our group set out for a nice dinner, again to the mall and a higher-end Italian restaurant.

Michael Toia

Friday arrived: departure day. Finishing a last breakfast, we bade friends goodbye, checked out, returned to the airport, inquired yet again. Aha! Our wayward bag awaited us. The twenty-five dollar bag fee paid for its transportation was now earned by the airline, albeit entirely too late. The parcel now retrieved, it was added to our remaining bags, and we checked in.

Ahh yes – the bag fee. Another twenty five dollars demanded and paid to return that wayward travel bag to home destination, a treatment similar in some respects to that offered by Sheri's, a bit less costly, and absolutely less enjoyable. Oh, well: that profession, tho not permitted in most of the country, remains legal in Nevada.

BRAKE BRAKE ONE TWO

I t was a long haul, from high school days to earning of a
bachelor's degree in science. Five years had elapsed. From a
teenager I grew to being a more mature young man. The study had
been interesting but quite challenging, and the fifth and last year
admixed both classwork and full time employment: college can be
expensive. But finally it was over, finished, and accomplished
debt-free as well.

At graduation there was but one of the female gender with
whom I had a close relationship, a love, a commitment. Her name
was Mom. That final work-and-study year seriously attenuated the
process of meeting and dating young ladies. Though time had now
come to begin an adult life, the prognosis was that of bachelorhood.
This had not been my desire, but rather what fate seemed to be
delivering. It was time to seek a remedy to the situation.

A call to an ex-girlfriend provided an update: she had in the
interim married, but passed on the name of a young lady, one of her
longtime friends, suggested I call, and further challenged that if I
did, I would marry her. I scoffed in disbelief, but her assessment of
the situation was far more accurate than mine.

I called. We dated. We married – all between June and December of that year.

Our church wedding was lovely, not overly elaborate, but wonderful, held in the dead of winter. Murphy – you know Murphy: the prophet of bad luck – dumped eleven inches of snow the night before. At seven AM my best man, Sid, rousted me from sleep. The ceremony was scheduled in a town several miles distant, rather hilly terrain intervening. He was, however, quite up to the task, having been reared a bit East of Buffalo, where eleven inches of snow is but a moderate dusting. In our neck of the woods it was on the cusp of decision: should schools and other events be closed for the day? A single additional inch would seal the deal, and the city would close, cancel the day for lack of interest.

Sid hurried me through breakfast, dressing, and in not too long we were in his auto and headed off, toward my intended's home town church. Father would bring my auto along later, mother driving the family car and following.

Now Sid and I had been chumming around a few years. He had been completing a hitch in the Navy when his family moved to town, and on his discharge we met, became inseparable friends, and best men at each other's weddings. He had been married six weeks earlier, and it was now my turn at the altar.

During our friendship we drove about those hills, together, summer and winter, and he taught me a lot of the tricks to get around and through rather "heavy" snow – heavy to me, a modest snowfall to him. So this trip was pretty much an experience we had already handled many times before. The wedding was set for two PM wedding. We arrived at the church at 9:30 AM. A tad early.

It was closed. Locked. We found instead a hotel dining room a few blocks distant, installed ourselves therein, had a bit of a snack with coffee, talked about our friendship and good times together. Unfortunately I had recently been offered, and accepted, a job as a scientist some four hundred miles to the East. We knew our friendship need survive without daily interaction, and survive it did with the help of two additional best friends: his wife, and my about-to-be.

The clock crept on, slowly but stubbornly. It would not be denied its programmed advance. We had a bit of lunch. I'm not sure how many times we had drained the shop's coffee pot that morning, but more than once, I would wager. A return to the church was now becoming imperative. We did so. It was still locked! A check with the parsonage found the minister unhurriedly preparing for the event. He, loaning us a church key – an honest-to-God door key to unlock the building, not the device so-named whose purpose in that age was to open beer cans –directed we enter, leave the door unlocked for guests and others to assemble, and told us where to wait as members of the wedding party. Those directions were carried out. Sid and I took up our assigned station.

One o'clock approached. The church was yet empty. No guests nor others had arrived. The snow seemed to have delayed everyone. And just a bit after, an elderly lady arrived, was the first to enter, and took a seat on the groom's side of the aisle. I went out to greet this visitor, my maternal Grandmother, who had traveled several hundred miles by train and taxi from an adjoining state. Why does the one who travels the farthest arrive first? Weird.

Two o'clock approached. The church was yet about empty. I consulted my wristwatch, nervously, wondering: when I had first proposed marriage, that darling young lady had turned me down. It took another month before she finally accepted. Now I agonized: had she come to her senses, realized she did not want to marry me after all, and this day would be one of those most sad, disappointing days of one's life – my life? But more guests and some members of the wedding party arrived. Still others were entering.

Three o'clock: still neither bride nor bridal party. I continued my self-doubt, fretting the whole time. I felt though I should just exit the rear door and slink off into a mood of gloom. But Sid would have none of it. He threatened bodily harm if I even began such an attempt. And he was right. As four o'clock approached, the bridal party finally began to assemble: bridesmaids, father of the bride, mother as well. The groom's ushers had all been in place at two. It appeared as if the ceremony would, in fact, occur.

Finally. Metaphorically speaking, "Someone put a nickel in the juke box." [20] The music began, the wedding party took up their designated positions. And there entered a small tot, walking the aisle toward the altar rail scattering flower petals. Completing her promenade, she took her seat.

A segue to the traditional bridal march brought the appearance of the father of the bride, escorting the most beautiful sight I had to that date witnessed. The ceremony commenced, continued, and concluded. I was too emotionally attached to comment on much else. And with a directed, permitted kiss of the bride, we were finally man and wife, woman and husband.

Many approached us, congratulating both. Toward the end of the hubbub the Reverend came to my new Mrs., saying there was need of his completing some necessary paperwork, and asked for the correct spelling of her complete legal name. She gave her first, middle, and family name – absent the new addition of mine. Reverend turned to me and said, "This is a little test I do with every bride I join in matrimony. You're going to have trouble with this one!" Trouble? Oh, Lord! Yes – interesting trouble. Fifty-eight years of it and counting. But it's been worth each and every second of it, bar none.

There followed a reception in the church main meeting hall. It, too, was lovely, but my mind was on other matters: the acquisition of a spouse, a young lady that I totally adored, how we would begin our new life, the honeymoon, the drive to our new residence four hundred miles distant, the snow, and on. In the course of events Sid came to me, quietly spoke, saying my now-brother-in-law and friends had calculated which route we would take, and were planning on driving that way, checking motels, and cause us a good bit of commotion on our first night together. I thanked him and mentally modified plans accordingly.

About nine-thirty we delegated the reception to others, took our leave. Father handed me the keys to my car, said her luggage had already been loaded therein along with mine. He had driven the car

---

[20] It was some time ago. A nickel sufficed then.

Michael Toia

up to the church. My bride and I said goodnight to one and all, entered the auto, and began a drive toward the main highway. Once there, I turned not East, the planned route, but Northwest, continued for about an hour, and arrived at a motel some forty miles North of town. It remained quiet. We finally had each other and began our life together, a wonderful life following a wonderful evening.

We departed late morning, shortly after plows removed the additional overnight four inches of snow from the parking lot, and took a parallel route to the East, a drive that took us from West-Central Pennsylvania toward the Poconos. Of course they closed the Poconos that time of year. Who cared? We had no need of crowds, just each other. I drove a few hours. Then my sweetie asked, "Would you want me to drive a bit?"

Well, it seemed like a good idea. I was a bit tired. She needed to get the feel of our – previously my – auto. I stopped, opened the door, stepped out and promptly fell on my kiester. It was quite icy and slippery, although the route was relatively level, with no menacing steep grades to negotiate. I made my way about the auto to her side, and she slid across to the drivers' side. I entered, closed the door. She settled in, looked down, then said:

"Why do you have two brake pedals?"

Oops ...!

She had learned to drive with an automatic transmission! Ours was stick-shift, a manual transmission. But learn she did, right then and there, and a bit later in life we acquired an International-Harvester Scout SUV. She became adept at handling its four-wheel drive, manual five-speed transmission *and* two-speed transfer case. She was a natural.

Ahh, yes – recollections. Warm, wonderful. It's as if all had happened just last weekend.

A TRINITY

W hy, I do not know. Bur at times people regard me as a god. I offer in proof thereof a trio of scenarios, my ascension to becoming yet another trinity, one god in three persons. My story, not meant in blasphemy but only as a comparison, is a parallel to Christianity.

First Person:

Lynn, a proper lady associate and member of a mutual fraternal group, was quite friendly, rather attractive, and worked in the computer programming or systems analyst field. Her firm had sent her on assignment to India for a spell, where I presume she did as most others would, picked up some of the flavor and culture of another society, its mannerisms, beliefs, routines, and so forth. She was a rather young professional woman, and I, an aged septuagenarian.

On her return, pleasant conversation around our group often turned to her experiences, her impressions garnered from the recent foreign travel. Most of us had never been to the country, and several had piqued interested in what she had to relate about the adventure and her impressions of that society.

My physique, quite overweight, reminds many of a major literary figure: Santa Claus. Apparently it also triggered Lynn's religious memory as well. She developed a kidding habit of approaching me, reaching out and rubbing my tummy while chanting, slowly, but in volume enough to be heard by all standing nearby, "B U D D H A – B U D D H A." This continued for a time. It was not terribly welcome, but unpleasantly embarrassing and somewhat irksome.

I did not wish to be a disagreeable, cranky old curmudgeon and grumble about the treatment, or be insulting, tho the thought occurred from time to time. I suppressed it because my general approach to life and associates is one of happiness and cheer: I've been granted quite a lot of both over the years, as spouse of my true love.

Lynn so proceeded yet again at an evening social gathering. A reaction formed right on the spot, without premeditation, with no intent at malice, as just a spur-of-the-moment commentary. I announced in slow, deep, resonant tones:

"I have become a god among women."

She, a deeply devout feminist, ceased finding further humor in the matter. We remained friends, although Lynn seldom approached me after that evening. We remained distant friends.

Ahh, yes –I had been, at least for a short time, a god, but alas! Not immortal. Shucks. I thought I was getting somewhere.

Second Person:

Associates experiencing difficulty at times become exasperated, look at me and say, "It's all *your* fault!" To end the argument, I agree. "Yes, it's *my* fault," then extend forth my right hand, palm up, and add, "I'll have my tithe now. Fifty percent."

The accuser stops, exclaims, "What! A tithe is only ten per cent!" I answer, "That's that wimp YAHWEH. HE takes ten percent. *I* take fifty percent. Pay up or shut up." The discussion ends.

At other times I walk into a room at work. Assembled co-workers see me, and say, "*Oh God - you here again?*" Now I look into the mirror daily, and do not myself see the resemblance. But it must be unmistakable. Consider the following logic: we Christians accept Jesus as God. One selection in our Methodist hymnal states that we want to be more like Jesus. Ask, and it shall be given unto you. It seems it has.

This situation, however, wanes at times, generally after shifts in work assignments, change of crew, or on retirement. My god in second person is again not immortal. Rats!

Third Person:

My wife, so delightful and charming a creature, my true love, sometimes gets involved in other matters while letting dinner on the stove just a trifle too long – not overly so, but the food develops a somewhat delightful crispiness to it, a change in texture, yet still delicious.

In one of our residences she and the smoke detector did routing battle. Time and again it sensed, then announced the dinnertime situation as was its duty. I still hear that oh-so-sweet voice *dratting* and *darning* the thing, the sound of a chair being dragged beneath it, her climbing aboard and removing the device from its nook on the upper wall just outside the kitchen area. She has yet to actually burn one out: after a reasonable airing and reinstallation, they all seem to work properly ... as is generally attested at the next meal's preparation.

Apres-battle, she calls me to dinner. She serves. She feels a bit sheepish, and apologizes with, "I'm sorry honey. Here's my burnt offerings." Frankly, I've become quite fond of the comment and anticipate it with a warm heart. The aroma of diner on the stove, followed by the detector's shrieking and her *dratting* and *darning*, are events I lovingly enjoy. I get a chuckle each and every time she greets me that way. I respond by reaching out to her, and absolve her of the sin by the laying on of hands. That remedy is always successful. I've come to fully understand and appreciate YAHWEH's desire for the same sort of offerings. And to appreciate more deeply the woman of my life.

This manifestation, this third person god that I have become, has taken on an immortality, at least as far as my life is concerned, and as far as this story progresses, carried by my spawned offspring beyond my demise into the future. At last: a god immortal I have become.

I offer here a post-script, a comment on God, the Christian Deity. As a Christian, I have been taught from before the time of continuity of memory that HE created heaven and earth, the stars and moon, and all manner of things that abound on the earth – the trees, animals, lakes, mountains, oceans, and on. That is, God has created everything.

Now when I shop, I examine items offered for sale. All carry the notation, "hecho en China" or its equivalent. So, logically, I have discovered:

God is Chinese!

Who knew?

THEATER

This is a piece condensed from afterthoughts and flights of fancy about an evening's entertainment. It's in the category of, "It ain't true, but shoulda been."

A dinner theater performance based on a murder mystery required audience participation. The plot was introduced, a member of the theater troupe was shot. It was not clear by whom. A roving detective, a cast member, came through the dinner floor with remote microphone, and engaged in conversation with one person seated at each table, visiting in turn all groups. Dependent on the particular theater-goers personality, various impromptu dialogs developed. Some were outgoing, engaging, while other quite shy and reticent patrons said little or nothing. Rover worked the crowd skillfully, kept the theme and entertainment going to the delight of all.

At one table sat an older senior citizen and three female companions. He was quite portly, largely balding with a pronounced bushy, gray beard and moustache. For all the world he reminded one of Saint Nick, just a bit out of uniform. In fact, very early in the performance the female lead of the troupe had called attention to him: " Santa Clause is with us tonight!" The spotlight danced across the crowd and came to rest upon him. One and all witnessed the gent.

Rover mercilessly polled the tables, skipping none. And as he approached "Nick," the theater music segued to the tune of *Here Comes Santa Clause, Right Down Santa Clause Lane."* Rover addressed Nick, who rose to his feet, and the following dialog developed.

Rover: "And good evening, Sir – who are you?"

Nick: "You no know? They know. Listen to music."

Rover: "By golly! You're Santa Clause! And who are these three ladies with you?"

Nick: "Groupies."

Rover: "Groupies! Where are they from?"

Nick: "Dunno. They dragged me in here."

The audience laughed a bit about the developing, ad-libbed story line.

Rover: "You're from the North Pole?"

Nick: "You nuts? Too cold. Winter there."

Rover: "South Pole?"

Nick: "Too crowded. Patagonia."

Rover: "Patagonia?!"

Nick was quite portly, rather tall, took on a menacing look and leaned deeply, overpoweringly, into the personal space of Rover, face to face, and in tough, teamster-like, slow threatening tones, said,

"You got *problem* with that?"

Rover: "Oh, no – no – just surprised, that's all. Why Patagonia?"

Nick backed off to his previous stance.

Nick: "Quiet. No crowds. Paparazzi illegal, shot on sight. No nosy people poking microphone into face. Decent Weather. Good work force. Low labor rate. Nice place. You visit sometime. Gonna love it."

Rover: "OK. I'll put it on my list. Now – who do you think committed the murder tonight?"

Nick: "Prob'ly Slasher."

Rover: "Slasher?"

Nick: "Spare reindeer. Bad dude. Always trouble. He the one. Sure."

With that, Rover thanked Nick and sashayed off to another table.

The show itself was adult fare, laced with much in the line of sexual connotations and double-entendres that brought forth roars of laughter from time to time. And when the performance was completed, the audience filed out, walking by the entire troupe who had lined up in the lobby area. Cast members greeted each patron and thanked them for their attendance. As Nick approached, the female lead did a bit more acting, gushing an "Oh, no – Santa Clause. Have I been naughty or nice? I'm in deep trouble, aren't I?"

And "Santa," amplifying the adult theme of the entire performance, looked at her, and in a reply made to be heard by all nearby, said, "You OK – sometime naughty is Nice."

LADY LUCK

S everal states operate a lottery system, a legalized gambling operation, as a means of generating revenue. Citizen hopefuls flock to licensed retail outlets, often grocery stores and mini-marts, to plunk down a few dollars for one or more lottery tickets. Generally each evening the television news has a short segment where some bingo-type balls with numbers affixed thereto are selected by a random process, the balls then arranged sequentially in a tray as they bounce out of the selector device. The sequence of four, five, six, or so numbers are displayed to the viewing audience and proclaimed to be the evening's lottery pick. If your ticket matches some of the numbers, you win a few dollars. If it matches all, you've hit the jackpot, often tens, or hundreds of thousands of dollars.

The odds of wining are not large. Quite the opposite. One is more likely to be struck by lightning. Most evenings there is no grand winner, and the "jackpot," the pool of money to be paid out to a grand winner in the future, grows. The system operates on the hope, the off-chance expectation, of a large payout, despite mountainous odds against it. But every month or so, more or less randomly, someone wins. Someone *must*, to fuel the desire that keeps the lottery running and ticket purchasing brisk. State-sponsored radio and TV advertising keeps interest up.

Our home state runs such a lottery. Their ads once featured a rather attractive-looking blond female that, to me, was on the very cusp of beauty. Just a bit more in the department of "looks," and she would be. A little less, and she would be somewhat homely. Of course her costume, makeup, and acting was done to convey precisely this appearance. This near-beauty, dressed as a fairy with a magic wand and crown, was billed as "Lady Luck" in the half-minute or so commercials.

In one period of non-jackpot payouts, a statistical "dry spell," the TV commercial saw Lady Luck visiting a fix-it shop, stating that her wand had lost some of its "zip," and was in need of a tune-up and polishing. She left it for servicing. And in the next several days the commercial saw her back at the shop, asking about it. The camera view was initially from the customers' side of the counter.

The counterman said the wand is not ready yet: its repair is a bit more challenging than first estimated. Lady Luck, a bit skeptical, furrowed her brow, and in lightly scolding tones, demanded, "You're not *playing* with that thing, are you?" Counterman, somewhat defensively and sheepishly, denied the charge with an "Oh – oh, no!"

As their dialog unfolded, the camera angle paned about to see the scene more from the counterman's side. It's then revealed that his lower body, the part initially hidden from view by the counter, had become that of a large chicken – suggesting that he *had* been playing with the wand.

This string of commercials went on for a week or two, but Lady Luck eventually recovered the wand, and a jackpot payout occurred. And in the course of time, the lottery ran statistically well, but hit another dry spell. Lady Luck reappeared. She addressed the TV viewer, lamenting that luck has been not too good recently, apologized by saying, "I got home the other night, a bit tired, set the wand on the sofa, made a cup of tea, and plopped down – right on top of it. Snap! Broke it in two."

She then added, "I thought of taking it back to the shop, but who knows what *that* might do. Fortunately, I'm an expert welder, so we'll have this thing up and running in no time."

The scene changed, showing views of the lottery process, the selection of the numbered balls, and the voice-over became that of a male announcer, exhorting the viewing public to keep on playing the lottery, extolling the great hope of winning not only several tens of dollars here and there, but of the jackpot and its current, somewhat elevated sum resulting from the dry spell.

And just at the end of the commercial, his voice was subdued, drowned out by that of Lady Luck, loudly and alarmingly exclaiming, "**Ouch!** That's **Hot!**" – another example of a commercial with "legs" carrying its message much father than usual.

TACKY

If I drop a thumbtack, how will it land? And why would I care? But I did. For a good reason.

Statistics, the mathematical study of chance, predicts such outcomes. For example, flip a coin. Will it be heads or tails? The chance of heads is about 50%. [21] Toss a die. There's one chance in six that it will show a three on its top face – or any other number from one to six, for that matter. And these play-scenarios, the tossing of a coin or a die, are often used in scholarly discussions about the odds of a future event's occurrence.

And so it was, as I read a technical article. Its author used the quite unusual analogy, the dropping of a thumbtack, to predict the result of a process the article discussed.

The tack has a smooth, lightly rounded head, and a sharp spike sticking out at right angles from its center. Dropped on a hard floor, it will stop bouncing in one of two ways: head on the floor

---

[21] It does, from time to time, come down on its edge. And if done outdoors, a bird might snatch it in flight, and it does not come down. These outcomes are so unusual we ignore them.

and the spike sticking straight up, or leaning over, the spike's point and the head's rim both touching the floor. The author said the process of which he was speaking had a probability, a chance, equal to the chance that a dropped thumb tack will wind up with its spike pointing straight up.

Hmmm? What is that probability, I wondered? And that led me into this story line.

Some doodling on paper and attempting to apply the laws of physics just got a bit confusing. I had a thumb tack in my desk drawer, so started tossing it up and letting it bounce onto my desk. I tabulated how many times it came down either way.

Then that metaphorical light bulb materialized, illuminated above my head: I could speed up this process with a few more tacks. A stroll to the company supply closet netted two boxes, 500 thumbtacks in each, and an empty mail tray. These in hand, I returned to my office, poured the thousand tacks into the tray, stepped out into the middle of the floor, and tossed the batch toward the ceiling with quite a "heft." It rained thumb tacks for a few seconds. And there I stood: in a minefield! I hadn't completely thought things through.

A dilemma! What to do? Well, by squatting down a bit, I was able to push the tacks gently aside without changing their spike up/down condition, and made a small tack-less area on the floor. Then prudence suggested marshalling the pointy, threatening ones to this area, and in so doing, gently sweeping the less dangerous, leaning ones along. That way, the field of tacks was separated into two growing piles.

When finished, I placed all of point-up tacks into the empty mail tray, and the others into the original two boxes. A trip to the supply room led me to the postage scale. The tacks from the tray were weighed, the weight noted, and then, with all tacks poured onto the scale, a total weight taken.

Aha! I had an answer to the question: what percentage would – or, in fact, did – come down pointy end up? It was the weight of the pointy ones divided by weight of all of them. I returned to my office with answer in mind, did the division, wrote the quotient on a Post-it, and pasted that on the page where the article posed the original question.

But, as a good scientist, I decided once again to repeat the experiment, particularly as I had a procedure worked out. I did. Tacks again rained onto my floor, the defusing process of sweeping the real threats to one side and the benign to another, produced a second result. Another weighing showed essentially the same percentage. This, too, was written on a second Post-it, and pasted on the article page next to the first.

While the experiment was being completed, a pile of thumb tacks in the mail tray and two open tack boxes nearby, my boss came into the office, asked what I was up to. I showed him the article, the comment by the author of the relative percentages, my results. He asked how I had done the experiment, and I filled him in. We discussed the matter. He fiddled with the mail-tray-full of tacks, the thousand, minus perhaps a few wayward ones here and there hiding beneath the desk or behind a filing cabinet.

He brought up an axiom of science: an experimental outcome, to be valid, must be performed by a differing researcher, and the results must agree. So, taking the tray, he walked to my door, stepped into the hallway, turned, threw the tacks ceiling ward, and with a good, somewhat maniacal, mocking laugh, said, "Do it again. See if you get the same answer!"

There I sat: tacks everywhere. On the floor. On my desk. On my lap. On my sleeve. A few in my hair. The de-fusing procedure became a tad more involved, invoking a bit more risk, but in about twenty minutes all had been collected in two piles. Using the original boxes and an ancillary container – the boss had absconded with the mail tray – I once again did the weigh-in, with an acceptably close result. We had scientific agreement!

Oh, yes – mea culpa! I forgot to tell you the answer. Well, to that I say – Bah! Go get your own thumb tacks! Or buy this book, seek me out for an autograph, and ask. *Then* I'll tell.

SMATHE

Field fatigues, at the time an OD shirt, trousers, block-type baseball cap, and black boots, completed with an M1 carbine rifle and an ammunition belt, was the uniform of the day. It differed from the modern Army field dress and appurtenances that developed over the intervening decades. And a proper soldier proudly projected a "spit-and-polish" image, everything in excellent order, clean to the point of excess. Boot shine, to be acceptable, had a black mirror-like finish. A true soldier "broke starch" each morning. [22, 23] Of necessity brass insignia and belt buckle had the highly polished, brightest possible appearance. Every part of the uniform was as clean and immaculate as could be accomplished.

Completing the picture, the ammunition belt held standard equipment: a first aid pouch, a canteen, ammunition pouches, and neatly tucked and circularly wrapped, taking on the look of a large tootsie roll, a poncho, lashed to the rear with spare boot laces. It

---

[22] In the day the Army was yet primarily men.

[23] Insertion of a foot caused the two halves of a pant leg, stuck together by a heavy starch laundering, to peel apart with a characteristic *schrrrch* sound.

rested in the small of the back. For most troops it was an item of uniform, had a specific function, but was rarely needed. To the elite, it was yet another item of adornment, tightly and precisely rolled, and waxed, exhibiting a neo-mirror-like shine.

We were STRAC troopers, members of the Strategic Army Corps, although as with much of military life, the acronym took on a more comically mocking mynorca, [24] or actually, two of them: "S**t! The Russians are Coming!" or "Stupid Troops Running Around in Circles." The being of a STRAC trooper was taken with quite some pride, and an extreme need for "spit and polish" became part of the fiber of a number of its elite. I tried. I met acceptable standards but was never a top trooper in that regard. Lieutenant Smathe was, and was highly regarded and envied by many.

This focus, on the pristine appearance of a man in uniform, is a good thing – but as with anything can taken to excess, produce a bias in one's thinking. Consider, for example, the firearms standing medal, with its three levels of accreditation: sharpshooter, marksman, and expert. Every trooper, STRAC particularly, was required to qualify with his assigned weapon. Not to have such a medal cast doubt on one's capabilities. We worked hard at it, and the spit-and-polish soldier settled for nothing less than the expert level. He spent many more days on the firing ranges than the demanded minimum. In any case, the expert medal itself became just another ornament, its function, to instill an "itch" in other troops to so achieve, forgotten.

In the course of usual daily operations, we remained on a military post, close to barracks and other buildings. One could find immediate shelter as a storm approached or raged. Never was there need of a poncho, its utility held for field maneuvers, field training exercises, where no convenient shelter might be available. In such occasions, several-week training exercises, we took shelter in large "command" tents. Our company had one such, containing tables and chairs, to implement the officers' field dining room.

---

[24] MYNORCA: ACRONYM spelt backwards, with an implied obvious meaning. Can be used as a noun or adjective

A particular Thursday the weather turned from warm and sunny at dawn, worsened quickly as the day proceeded. Mid morning thundershowers broke out. Rain fell: at times rather heavily. We deployed our ponchos and put them to their intended task. Twelve O'clock approached, as did meal assembly time. Company officers trooped individually into the mess tent, shed their rain gear as best could be done, wrapped them up wet to reduce bulk, but kept them handy to permit return to duty in a half hour or so.

Enter Lieutenant Smathe, soaked to the bone, appearing as a man just snatched from the throes of a drowning. No part of him escaped the attention of the storm. He greeted all, commenting on the wind and rain. The company commander – the CO – commenting on his condition, asked: "Lieutenant! Why are you not wearing your poncho?" To which Smathe replied, "I couldn't find it, Sir. It's probably back in my quarters. The following dialog transpired:

CO: "Lieutenant!"

Smathe: "Sir?"

CO   "Take off your ammo belt!"

Smathe did so.

CO: "Hold it up high!"

Smathe did so.

CO: "What's that thing rolled up and laced onto it?"

Smathe: "Well, doggone! So *that's* where it went!"

Yes, just another ornament. Sometimes they do have other functions. We had a good laugh, Smathe best of all, I believe.

THE FITTEST

An old commercial exhorts, "A mind is a terrible thing to
waste!" Twisted a bit to comment on my life-long problem
with obesity, it becomes, "A waist is a terrible thing to mind."
Before existing to age six, my body was quite frail. It had
acceptable height and a normal skeletal form over which was
stretched a membrane of skin, with normal protrusions as arms,
legs, etc. This worried Mom and Dad.

Vaguely do I recall those days: a dislike of eating. Food and
meals simply had no appeal. A visit to the family doctor,
concerned about my low weight, produced the diagnosis: Infected
tonsils. A bit of a hospital stay followed, where those little doo-
dads and the rest of me parted company. That I recall rather
vividly, the coming out of the ether anesthesia, the awful headache,
the pain in my throat. Mom and Dad were at the bedside.

Our family was Roman Catholic, as was the hospital. My first
words, in a fog of semi-consciousness were far from kind. They
invoked in a betrayed, angry manner the name of the Lord, quoting
something about their lying to me, that this operation would not
hurt. It did. And left a lasting impression, likely amplified by a

slap across the face delivered by some female member of the Zorro family, or at least so dressed. She was a mean lady, a nurse/nun. One slap did it. Dad caught her arm, said not many, but severely stern and threatening, words indicating that if she attempted to do so again, he would remove her arm and place it in his trophy room as a memento, and deposit the remainder of her body in the local river.

Recovery came soon enough, and we were once again home. I do remember thereafter discovering a fondness for a local delicacy. We lived just up and around two bends of the river from a factory whose large, ornate, brick smokestacks held a giant "57" sign. To this day, as with most true Pittsburgh natives, ketchup is that delicacy, and no meal is complete in its absence. And recently, some seventy years after my first delight at its taste, my lifelong best friend commented, "Do you still have that disgusting habit of eating ketchup on fig newtons?" I was taken aback. Disgusting? Why? Doesn't everyone eat them that way?

But back to my youth. Time went on. I grew. Ketchup played, and still does, a large role in my life. It delivers comestibles to the taste buds in an inexplicable manner. Mom's meat loaf was a heavenly, wonderful mouthful, as were mashed potatoes, always having a rather heavy red coloring on my plate. About the same time ground black pepper found its way, delightfully so, onto and into my meals.

That ketchup and black pepper, yet to this day exquisite condiments, turned a trick: weight gain. My body finally developed something between its bones and its skin. Some muscle set in. But unfortunately, so did flab. A few years aprez-hospital, I had gained reasonable weight, and in a few more was a bit overweight. I yet recall a statistic from our wedding day. My bride, beautiful beyond compare, was about as frail as I once had been. She stood three inches less than my height of a tad under a fathom. My weight was on the quite beefy side, one hundred ninety-six pounds, and hers precisely half that.

Several months passed. The Army called: they wanted me` to report, and it was done. Earlier ROTC training had placed me in an experimental program, leading to becoming a pilot of small observation aircraft and helicopters. I had little interest in such things, but had been drafted into the program.

The day came to report to duty. A physical exam stated, "three pounds overweight, remediable." I had gained a bit of weight, thanks to the effects of ketchup and black pepper, and that of my sweet bride. I could reapply in six months. In the interim word arrived that three of my fellow ROTC aviators had been sent off to Vietnam, shot out of the sky, and killed. It then dawned on me that perhaps there is another twist to a famous quote, viz.: "Survival of the *fattest*." Wife and I decided that the suggested three-pound remedy not be attempted, and concept of flight school thus be dashed. I continued to gain weight, a few pounds a year.

On reaching the late forties, my figure approached that of Santa. And in the early fifties, it approached something else: doctors' offices, more and more frequently. I've had a half dozen or so doctors, all suggesting some weight loss. And well-meaning friends did the same. A few have asked, "Doesn't your doctor suggest you lose weight?" I reply, utilizing a comment of comedian George Burns: "Yes. Three of them. Two are dead, and the third don't look too good."

Doctors are good, honorable. Why, I'd trust my life to one. Come to think of it, I do! And on several office visits, they've called attention to a chart on the wall, showing a relationship between height and weigh, the *height-weight* chart. One fella was rather a disciplinarian. He demanded, "Look at that chart! Look closely. What does it tell you?" I followed instructions, and discovered that I was woefully short.

Yes, I am obese. Do I want to lose weight? Of course. And I do, on and off, akin to Mark Twain's comment on giving up smoking. Losing weight is easy. I've done it a thousand times.

I've reached age eighty plus. Obesity is a curse, leads to a shorter life span. But I've discovered wisdom in that "Survival of the fattest" conclusion.

RITIN'

W ith two score and several years experience managing staffs of engineers, I've edited, corrected, contributed to, and composed many a technical report. The process illuminates, often painfully so, the limited vocabulary and writing skills commonly attributed to so-named techno-geeks. They have good minds, many edging on brilliancy, and a command of their profession, but are limited in others. As a technocrat, I, too, have limits: don't ask me to cook dinner: we'll starve!

These limits often express themselves in an engineer's writings, the composition of a sentence, paragraph, and overall story. Most can read, understand, and compose complex diagrams of the space shuttle, but are baffled in construction of the simple diagram of a sentence, properly illustrating the subject, object, descriptive adjectives of either or both, the action verb with its adverbial attributes, and Oh, Lord! Don't ask them to handle two or more dependent or independent clauses. Consequently, their writing trends to confusion, repetition, misstatement of tenses, and logical contradictions, resplendent with miss-spelt words.

While attempting over the several years to put a sense of order into their written wilderness, I've composed a short list of guides offered as assistance to those struggling with the burden. Each point, in an attempt at humor, is a list of sentences or statements purposely violating the rule it conveys.

So, without further fanfare, I offer a:

RITIN GIDE
FOR INJUNEARS

Rules to ritin gud Inglish

"Six munce ugo eye kudnt evn spel injunear – an now eye are one."

The rules violated below are guides for those who become baffled or befuddled about their points:

1. Prepositions are not to end sentences with.

2. Don't never use double negatives. (That's a no-no.)

3. Remember to not split infinitives.

4. On preparing good reports, participles should not dangle.

5. The "i before e" rule has weird exceptions.

6. When enumerating sections and sub-sections, remember:
   (a)   If there is an (a), there must be a (b).

7. It is said, "The final punctuation mark is typed before the final quote mark"!

8. One thought, one paragraph. If you need to introduce a new thought, use a separate paragraph. Most text editors will check your spelling …

9. Be <u>clear</u>, <u>concise</u>, and <u>complete</u>. These qualities of communicating about things were first introduced for composition of messages which were intended to be trans-

mitted by radio – I was in the Signal Corps at the time – so as to make sure the message could be understood by its intended recipient, who might, after all, really need the information in the communication, whether it came to him verbally, by teletype, carrier pigeon – yes, the Signal Corps did actually use carrier pigeons, except that they seemed to have eaten the last one somewhere in Korea, as the pigeon service did not survive the Korean conflict – could it be that pigeons are a delicacy in Korea? I bet that's exactly what happened, come to think of it! An interesting thought …

10. Pronouns: he or she shouldn't use them to excess, or it will confuse them about that: they would understand better if it was written without them.

I rest my case –

P.S. Rule 3 is so frequently and blatantly violated today: to not use it is rather the acceptable norm, while not to use it has fallen to desuetude. I have coined a new word, a noun, describing the process: the infinisplitive.

A TREE

S am, my father's best friend, was almost family. Our homes were a few blocks apart in a small, well-established suburban town. The streets were paved with brick, block, or at times blacktop, and large, steel-grey slate slabs paved the sidewalks on either side. A several-foot wide strip of land between the curb and the walk was devoted to the cultivation of shade trees, many of which were quite mature.

The trees possessed an interesting legal property. Alive, their ownership was that of the town, who provided care and maintenance. But when one died, its ownership was transferred to the property in front of which it stood. And it came to pass: a very mature oak in front of Sam's house succumbed, relinquished efforts at further life, and commended itself and its funeral arrangements to Sam.

A dead tree of this size is a bit of a hazard. It could fall on Sam's house, a neighbor's house, or onto a passing auto or pedestrian. The town ordinance required that, once ownership had been ceded to the property owner, the latter had a few months to remove the thing. Sam set about seeking contractors who could perform the task. Their estimates about floored the man: it would take more than a month's salary to pay for the work.

Now neither Sam's nor our household was one of very comfortable means. We were what was termed lower - middle class citizens, common laborers. Sam held a position as a maintenance man caring for the county roads, and father worked in the local foundries. We lived, quite often, paycheck to paycheck, with very little cash reserve. Sam needed removal of the tree: it was done, and the crew that did so took a down payment deposit, then arranged for Sam to make monthly payments to complete his obligation. Sam did so.

The spring following, the town sent a crew along to plant a replacement tree, a little thing hardly fifteen feet tall. It lasted that season, even though it seemed to thirst a bit in the heat of summer. It shed its leaves on schedule, but failed to leaf out the following spring. The following midsummer its possession was passed to Sam, who was able to effect its removal armed with simple hand tools. I believe he used a common carpenter's crosscut saw to fell the thing: its trunk was hardly three inches in diameter.

Spring arrived yet again. The town sent another crew, to replace the replacement tree. It, too, went through its normal annual growth cycle, shed its leaves come fall, but also succumbed to the throes of winter. By late spring it was obviously a goner, and come fall Sam cut it down, as it was now his.

The cycle repeated itself a few more years. The town finally gave up the project of replacing that original old, grand oak tree dating from a hundred years or so earlier, back to the very beginnings of the town. Apparently something got into the soil at the base of that old oak, poisoned it, such that no new tree could survive.

In a private conversation I overheard between father and Sam, I concluded why the spot was infertile. Sam tended the tree and each fall gave it a feeding to help it along, a feeding of material used for winter road work: rock salt. He reasoned that, if the tree, dead, was his, he wanted it of manageable size, one he could himself handle, with no need of an expensive, professional crew.

There's a moral here. Don't penalize citizens in caring for public property. The latter will fare far better if, instead, you reward them for its care.

Michael Toia

THUNDER

I n every school system a student or two excel in math and the sciences, usually go on to college, an advanced degree, and a profession wherein they becomes recognized exerts. I recall three such in our small school, in a sequence of three years, our science kids, mutual friends, a senior, junior, and sophomore in that order. They were the physics and chemistry's stars in their respective times at bat, and the science teacher's assistant in preparing and conducting classes.

An incident concocted by Roger, the senior science kid of that year, had an unexpected reaction. The school band prepared their annual late spring concert. I don't recall the particular musical piece, but it involved the sound of an approaching storm. Roger found that, by lifting and gently shaking a rather large piece of sheet steel, it voiced the sound of thunder. The harder it was shaken, the fiercer the sound.

A proper physicist, Roger knew as we all do that light travels much faster than sound. We're trained to begin counting off the seconds between a bright lightning flash and its thunderclap. Five seconds: it's a mile off. Ten: two miles. One, with very loud thunder, it's close. Simultaneous, with the smell of ozone: you're lucky to be alive!

Roger set up a flood lamp backstage near the steel sheet, and drafted an assistant to control the lamp. The intent was to mimic the approaching storm, not only with the sound, but with light flashes as well. I was that assistant. We practiced after school several times. And by golly, it was a magnificent effect. A few bystanders were asked for comment, and reported it really made them feel there was an approaching storm.

The calendar advanced: the day of the concert arrived. It was a warm, pleasant spring day in the early nineteen fifties: the hall had no air conditioning – believe it or not. Its main exterior windows were open and a light, pleasant breeze wafted through the place. Who *needed* air conditioning? The atmosphere was perfect.

In early evening the audience gradually filed in and took seats. A goodly number of town folk came out to support our musicians, many by a short stroll from their homes. And the concert began. The performance was really quite good: our musicians were a nicely accomplished and talented troupe.

The show proceeded: the finale, the piece with storm sound effects, began. Our physicist and I were in position backstage. On cue, a flash of light, several seconds delay, and a light rattle of that steel sheet. The sound of thunder from afar wafted across the audience.

The music became more agitated. The light flashes became a bit more intense, longer lasting. The fake thunder followed more closely thereafter, with increasing intensity. Nearing the piece's theatrical climax, the sound and light effects ran much more vigorously, light flashes admixed with thunder, the sheet being tortured to a good extent, issuing forth the sound of a furious storm approaching. It was magnificent! Our physicist had outdone himself.

With the tempo approaching *con fucco,* [25] the audience became psychologically involved. Many were visibly concerned and agitated. And as the climax approached, about half rose to their

---

[25] Musician's score term: *"with fire!"*

feet and made for the door, attempting to outrun the storm on the way home! 'Twas too much of a good thing ...

TORPEDO

A young lady studied well, achieved good grades in the county school system. Her parents had moved to that particular area to have advantage of its reputed excellent educational opportunities, and that was found to be true. The lass graduated with a high standing in her class, applied to a state technical college, and was accepted. She continued her studies, and in five years earned a baccalaureate in Mechanical Engineering. Shortly after graduation she was found employed by the U. S. Navy, working in the area of Undersea Warfare.

The Navy operated a program similar to that in large industries. They rotated their new hires about, giving them several month's experience in various work areas so the newbie gets a feel of what the overall operation entails, and might either develop a desire, or a noted special aptitude, to be placed in a particular line of work. To that end our subject found herself at different naval bases for her first few years on the job. One four-month assignment was to the Naval Undersea Warfare Center at Keyport, Washington.

Keyport was a continent's width separate from home, her old friends and parents. The cellphone played a central role in family life. Calls to home occurred a few times each week. She related the experience of living in a somewhat different environment, more at a rainforest during some seasons, the state's ferry boat system to get around on the Sound, the sights and aromas of Seattle, the mountains, all of which were sufficiently different from home as to be worthy of considerable comment.

More conversation concerned her first work experience, the job, co-workers, interesting assignments. At the time she was assigned to work on torpedo technology. In one call home, she asked for Dad, also an engineer, and said excitedly, "Dad! I got to take a torpedo apart today!" It was to her a memorable point in on-the-job training. But that assignment came to an end, and she returned to her home town, working again at the Washington Navy Yard in the District of Columbia.

There were other assignments, one to Naval Undersea Warfare Center, Newport, Rhode Island. While there she caught the attention of a young chap, a fellow engineer, and they dated, on and off, for some time. Her assignment ended; she returned again to the Navy Yard. And on an evening's visit to her parents' home, she said, "Keyport called. They want me to come back and work there!" This was, of course, quite a flattering comment on her abilities. But Dad kiddingly answered, "Yeah. You took their torpedo apart. They want you to put it back together again!"

But Newport won out. She and her former date from the area carried on a long-distance romance for many a month, until she arranged a transfer back to that station, and shortly after, Mom and Dad with older sibling and son-in-law found themselves in a church on Cape Cod, where Dad gave youngster away, gaining in the process another son-n-law.

Oh, by the way – that lass is my talented and beautiful younger daughter, and mother of a likewise beautiful granddaughter. These are some favorite memories. < ... sigh ... >

Epilogue

With this anthology of threescore recollections, and the first threescore in my earlier work, *Frog Tongues etc.,* I may have run out of memory space in my aging brain, itself at fourscore plus one years. It has been a wonderful life, endowed with many interests and curiosities, a soulmate wife of fifty-eight years and counting, two beautiful daughters, two sons-in-law, each the father of a granddaughter. The wellsource of further works based on actual life's experiences may have run dry, or at least low. Can I find further recollections to share? Time will tell, if the Good Lord provide me a bit more of it. But thank you for having made my countless, enjoyable hours at the keyboard worth more than simple self-amusement. God bless and keep you, dear readers, and accept my appreciation. Without you I am but an isolated island, remote and disconnected from the world.

Michael Toia   Christmas 2018   Culpeper VA

www.ingramcontent.com/pod-product-compliance
Lightning Source LLC
Chambersburg PA
CBHW070001120726
47909CB00003B/773